The Deep Whatsis

PETER MATTEI is a writer and director working in both theatre and film, and has written pilots for HBO and other networks. *Love in the Time of Money* was his first feature film, which he wrote and directed. The script was developed at the Sundance Filmmakers Lab in 1998, and was inspired by Arthur Schnitzler's play *La Ronde*. He lives in Brooklyn.

PETER MATTEI

The Deep Whatsis

The Friday Project
An imprint of HarperCollins*Publishers*
77–85 Fulham Palace Road,
Hammersmith, London W6 8JB

www.harpercollins.co.uk

A Paperback Original 2013

1

A catalogue record for this book
is available from the British Library

ISBN: 9780007524358

Printed and bound in Great Britain by Clays Ltd, St Ives plc

MIX
Paper from
responsible sources
FSC™ C007454

part one

The intern from the edit house is so drunk she is trying to take her skin off. At least that's what it looks like. She is already half-naked and is grabbing at her flesh trying to find the edge of the Threadless T-shirt that she lost half an hour ago. I don't remember her name.

"What are you doing?" I ask her as she pulls at her body, but it is no use, she can't hear me and if she can she doesn't understand.

Certain people when they drink too much they get an idea in their head and then it forms a kind of feedback loop in which the thought just repeats itself over and over, as if their brain is trying to grip on to something, anything, for dear life, because all of reality is slipping into the void. Megan? Morgan? Caitlin? Finally she speaks and her answer is she wants to take her T-shirt off because she likes to sleep naked, she's going to sleep now, it's one of the checkboxes of her still-forming self, sleeping in the nude, it's who she is, she sleeps in the nude in her sleeping bag even in winter, that's what she is saying to me over and over out of nowhere in the dark, so I just say good night and turn the lights off. She keeps babbling and looking at me with such a confused sense of joy that I want to laugh, so I do laugh.

Then I go into the bedroom and get a pillow and go into the bathroom and get the little trash-biny thing. I slide the pillow under her head and I put the trash-biny thing next to her and I tap her shoulder and point to the thing and explain to her that if she needs to barf she should barf in that and not on the floor, if possible, especially not on the pillow—it's Icelandic eiderdown.

She looks up at me and smiles and then she passes out.

Intern is extremely cute, alright, granted, her face at least, no question, it's like God smiling on sunshine, and she's cool, she quote unquote gets it, but still I plan that after this morning's pretend-awkward good-bye, which hopefully will happen in a mere couple of hours, to never see her again. For the moment however she is totally crashed and it's around 6 AM and I'm not really tired, which may have something to do with the stimulants we were ingesting at the bar where we met.

"What's up?" she said as I turned around, spun really, why I'm not sure, sloshing a double Rittenhouse rocks in my right hand. I was meeting this friend of mine, Seth Krallman, playwright turned pot dealer turned yoga guru, but he was blowing me off, what a surprise.

"Don't I know you?" she said.

"No," I said, never having seen the girl in my life.

"Yes, yes I do know you," she said. "You got the tuna." And then she told me it was she who brought the big sashimi platters into the editing session for us at lunchtime, the Viva Paper Towel editing session at the edit house where she worked, and she remembered me because I requested the Oma Blue Fin, rarest and most expensive of fish. It was like ninety dollars a roll and I barely touched the thing.

"I thought it was pretty lame," she said. "For the price."

"That's cool," I said. "Do you always eat people's leftovers?"

"Do you always waste really expensive food that is a) on the endangered list and b) caught by slave labor?" she asked, cocking her head to the earnest side and waiting for an answer.

"Um, I'm looking for a friend of mine," I said.

"No you're not," she said.

"No?"

"No, you're buying me a drink, aren't you?"

Maggie Mallory Margot is an intern at Unkindest Cuts, and I posted a slew of financial services commercials there two years ago so they owe me "big time." I'm not saying they told her she had to go home with me—I think she did that for her own reasons and because she drank too much, thanks mostly to my largesse. Now, sleeping there, she looks a bit more fleshy than I remember, curled up on the floor, pale, motionless. But, I must say, she's quite good looking: I make a mental note that she probably ranks in the upper third quadrant of girls I have ever had quasi-sexual relations with in terms of physical attractiveness; when you look at her in a certain light or from a certain angle, she's feral, and her eyes cradle a syrupyness you can almost taste. What would Howard Roark say about her? He was no writer but would always do something, something bold and innovative, writing being the opposite of that. I tap a note into my phone: "idea for short film, what if Howard Roark gave a TED talk?" I think about wanking but I don't.

Then I decide not to go back into my bedroom, because I can't sleep and because I want to make sure she doesn't wake up and steal something from me. So I sit down at my desk in the living area and take a look at the latest draft of the screenplay I am writing, which is called either GAME THEORY or KILL SCREEN or MAD DECENT—I haven't decided yet. I've been writing it for three years and I am still trying to figure out the inciting incident, which is the most important thing, at least according to some book I bought in LA when I lived there. Every guy in advertising is working on a screenplay they will never complete but I have more drive and discipline than most so maybe I will, although I am still on page two.

For the name of my main character I chose my own name, which is Eric Nye, and my own age, which is thirty-three, and my own hometown, which is Canfield, Ohio. I think that is a good touch. I think they call it self-referential.

I rewrite the opening sentence a few times and mostly I stare at the screen, adjusting my hard-on, which is perpetual for medicinal reasons, at least that is my theory, then I realize that the sun is coming up over the Williamsburg Bridge, which you can see outside my triple-pane window. Suddenly I can smell something funny and I go into the living area and sure enough she has upchucked—on my throw rug, believe it or not, which she managed to pull toward her and scrunch up to use as a pillow because she rolled off the nineteen-hundred-dollar St. Geneve one that I had provided for her.

I wake her up and she's a bit more cogent than before and so I walk her into the bathroom and turn the shower on and stick her head under it. Poor sad little girl, whatever will become of you? Then I dry her off and hand her the T-shirt and give her a bottle of Voss to wash her mouth out with. Her beauty has been fairly well line-itemed at this point, and I am not happy to report that she is even more sexy when 50 percent clothed. When she finally gets dressed and exits with a halfhearted wave of shame I jerk off, take my pills, and call a car service.

I fire people. It's my job.

But not only do I can them, in the process I help them, or should I say I wake them up, or I should say I take the time to write for them an honorable if not epic death, a death more dramatic and meaningful than the one they would otherwise be entitled to.

See, I was hired to "clean house" here at Tate, the ad agency in New York City where I am the Chief Idea Officer. I was brought in to create a culture of innovation and creativity, meaning get rid of the dead wood, shitcan the old and the slow and the weak, and that's what I'm doing, because it's my job.

At first it was something I dreaded. I knew I was being paid handsomely to be the one to blame, the one who does the Dirty Deed, but still, it was distinctly not cool. Then I grew up.

I read on page 334 of *The Fountainhead* where Howard Roark, say, cuts his own testicles off with a fork in front of his cousin or something, I don't remember, not that exactly, but he does some extremely fucked-up shit that is totally ridiculous but in the end is worth it. That hit me when I read it. So after firing a handful of pathetic art directors and copywriters in their forties and fifties my attitude changed. I realized that my problem with this aspect of my job was purely in my head and that if I were to be totally honest with myself I would admit that there was something heroic about it. The thrill of the hunt, I guess. I had my prey cornered, I had the HR Lady watching me (I call her Lady but she wasn't much older than me; tall, half-Korean—she lives on Diet Coke, coffee, and wine), and I had my sentence to speak, which thankfully she had written and rehearsed with me: *"I'm very sorry to say this but we're going to have to let you go."* That sentence was like a quiet little knife in my hands, a hand-painted bespoke artisanal elephant gun loaded and cocked and all I had to do was open my mouth and speak it, destiny would take its course, there was nothing anyone could do. The aftermoment would hang there in the air like steam, and the HR Lady would look at my now-finished and cold-sweating prey with fake sympathy but really I knew what she was thinking, she was thinking she was in the presence of a hard-boiled killer and it turned her on.

Once I gave in to understanding the simple truth about human existence I began enjoying the primal beauty and manifest joy of the kill. I began to turn it into an elaborate ritual. The act wasn't exactly the same thing as a hunt because the prey had no chance to escape, to run away and survive, as they do in the wild. A different metaphor comes to mind. Last year I was dating a woman, a model who lived in LA, and we went to Barcelona for a long weekend. On Sunday afternoon we went to the bullfight. She objected to this because sport bulls were on the PETA list and she spewed some line of rote nonsense about the cruelty of it and for the most part I bought into that. Of course I was also hoping to get blown one more time before we flew home.

"Think of it as anthropology," I said. "Think of it as a window into another world." And I suppose it was another world, in the way that, well, consider the care and patience that a serial killer will take with the body of his victims, or a medical examiner with a corpse, there is something horrific about it and honorable at the same time, like a sky burial. And the bullfight is not at all a sport, it is a dance, a performance art piece that originated on Spanish ranches and farms, or so I read online although I might be making that up. The bull is going to die regardless because it is going to be slaughtered for food, and so the matador honors his meal by risking his life in the ring, finally terminating it while leaping in midair, his groin exposed to the bull's horns. The whole thing was pretty gay but at the same time also undeniably deep I thought.

So that's how I began to think of my job. Sure, I could just follow my marching orders to the letter, call them into my office, shake my head, look at the floor, say my sentence, squeeze their hands, offer my help in finding them a new position somewhere, which we both knew was bullshit, let's get a drink sometime, dude, we'll miss you around here, the fucking bean counters up my ass we had no choice you're not alone, and so on. I could kill them the way we kill chickens in slaughterhouses, in some kind of dehumanized way, and they have no idea what's happening until the moment of their death, if at all, if a chicken even knows what death is, does she? Or I could send them out with the art and grace and dignity of a really good *commedia*, a good long bloody scene, replete with angels, demons, and clowns. They could be unwitting losers or they could be stars, and it was up to us, together, we were doing this as a team. But I was the one at the helm, with my year-long schedule of layoffs, my Outlook calendar entries, invites, and alerts. Outlook was my faena, my sword.

One of the hallmarks of Western industrial society is death segregation, the separating of the dying and the dead away from the masses and into so-called professional circles: medical practitioners, police, undertakers, military contractors. Some philosophers think this has resulted in neurosis if not psychosis; the exploits of Nazi Germany come to mind if not all of the pornography industry. Where am I going with this? I am bringing death back from the over-anesthetized margins, that's my mission, my purpose, and it is bigger than right-sizing the creative department on behalf of the shareholders of the holding company that owns the holding company that owns the company that employs me. I am exaggerating and ritualizing the methods of corporate termination for all humankind, for posterity; I have created a new art form.

But mostly I'm just trying to get my bonus.

That morning, after I called my building's concierge service and had them clean up Intern's puke and toss my eight-hundred-dollar Dalai Lama Edition Tibetan throw rug in the trash, the car service brings me to the office just before 8 AM. I sign the voucher and go inside, flashing my ID quickly as I pass the security cameras and monitors and the sign that says YOU ARE BEING VIDEOTAPED. I hadn't slept that night more than thirty minutes but it doesn't feel that way to me; I feel fine, in fact I feel great, of course I am still high as a kite. I know it will get uncomfortable at some point later in the day when I have to tell the editorial company where she works that we will be taking our business elsewhere because their work is "sub-standard," but for the moment I don't have to deal with it. I go into my office and shut the glass door and crank up my iTunes and listen to this Girl Talk remix of a Deadmau5 track produced by Pretty Lights and re-remixed by Devon Aoki: I'm lying but it's something like that. I am sure my enjoyment of this so-called music comes from the fact that I know these tracks are bootlegs, sent to me by a music company (called Earwig) that is trying to get into business with us, and so I am one of a handful of people on the planet who have them, and that is flattering, it would be to anyone. Although this story about them being rare bootlegs is probably not true, it's probably just the line of *mierda* the music house gave me to make me feel extremely good about myself, which would translate down the line into more money for them. Everything is seduction, everything is sexual in the end, even the passcode to an FTP download site. I put on my Beats-by-Dre headphones and listen to the track. It's really boring.

All forms of entertainment product have at their roots a base reason for being, a simple consumer benefit. If you ladder up to it, you see that certain things exist to make you frightened, for example, so that you can vicariously experience primal terror and survive it in the (relative) safety of a mall, endorphin rush as much a part of the experience as the popcorn. For millions of years Man lived with constant fear, in the wild, there were real monsters in the dark, things that would tear your head off and eat it while your eyes were still functioning, and we still need those neurons to fire now and then or they atrophy; this is a multibillion-dollar industry called movies and not to be confused with that other fear-based industry called politics. Or in the case of music, gangsta rap, the ultimate benefit is that it makes you feel empowered sexually when you listen to it, although if you are white and grew up in the suburbs like me fear is also a factor: again, I can experience this in the safety of my home or car, not on the actual Streets. And so it is a testosterone inducer, it has the same effect as the patch that ball-less guys are supposed to stick under their arms. The other chief benefits of entertainment properties are wish fulfillment and stress release (also known as comedy).

My calendar isn't particularly full today. A few boring meetings in which I will listen to some of our industry's least-talented creatives attempt to impress me with their awful, so-called ideas, and I will nod, pretend to hate them all, and say things such as "Do you really think this is the best you can do?" or "Do you really believe that bringing me work like this is going to help you keep your job?" They will always answer the same way, hemming and hawing and finally agreeing that there must be a better idea out there somewhere, and then I will just stare at them with feigned contempt for their vain struggle toward greatness which, deep down, none of us really cares about.

"If this isn't your very best work, why are you showing it to me?"

"If you were me, what would you say to you?"

There would never be a reply to that one. I don't think they could tell that the contempt was there in me, really. And I don't mean to say it was completely real, most of it was not, it was an act. I do have actual contempt for them but it has nothing to do with their advertising skills because I barely even regis- tered what it was they were showing me. I couldn't care less. I have contempt for them because I have contempt for this en- tire industry, myself included. Some business writers say that you don't motivate people by putting them down but I wasn't trying to motivate them, I was trying to de-motivate them. I was going to have to fire half of them anyway, so why would I want them to do a good job? Why would I want to meet their kids? On the other hand, if I were to motivate them and they did a better job and then I fired them, that would be even more confusing to them, which would provide some additional absurdity-enjoyment to me, and to the universe at large. I sup- pose I don't bother to motivate them because I am just too lazy to care whether or not anyone's pain or dramatic arc is fully maximized. After all, this isn't about me, I'm not the center of the universe, I'm just a cog in a larger wheel.

Around 1 PM I go to lunch by myself at Faco, which is a Mediterranean seafood restaurant specializing in Aegean shellfish prepared in wood-fired ovens. It is not far from the office. I sit at the bar, get the pan-seared octopus and the baked spinach and a $124 bottle of Sancerre. I have my laptop with me and look over the opening of my screenplay. It sucks. I stare at the octopus, but I don't touch it for some reason, possibly because of how irritated I get by the waiters swarming around me, creating a vortex of ingratiating fantasy: hey, look, we're all billionaires. The wine, the lack of sleep, and my thoughts wandering back to the night before contribute to making me feel unfocused, I can't get any work done. I get up and leave a 44 percent tip. As I walk out my iPhone buzzes and I see there is an SMS from a 347 number I don't recognize.

hey you
don't remember much un4tunatly
sorry about the !@#$!
u mad @ me?

How did she get my number? I delete the text. It's possible she looked at my phone when she was at my house—I vaguely recall setting it on my Ligne Roset dining table where she could have perused it—but she seemed far too drunk to have memorized a ten-digit number. Why am I feeling twinges of desire all of a sudden? I dial my assistant and she puts me through to the head of our production department—his name is Tom Bridge—and I tell Tom to pull the plug on Intern's edit house after the Viva gig and if they ask why tell them it's because of This Goddam Fucking Economy.

Henry Graham's name had been on the master termination list since the day I arrived. Because he had a good relationship with one of our medium-sized clients it was delicate and so HR Lady and I agreed to fire him in six months and we posted it in the spreadsheet, which was on Google Docs, and into the Outlook calendar. That would give us time to find a reason other than the fact he was forty-eight years of age and had been at Tate for years and was nearing the time when he could take a small pension; one of my mandates was to not let any more employees reach their vesting date. When I was hired I had sat down with HR Lady and we did the math, made a chart of all the people in the department—there were eighty-six of them at the time, a number which now strikes me as strange—and we figured out which ones would stay and which ones would get the sack in the coming fiscal. In order to get my bonus I had to trim the department by at least 50 percent. That's forty-three people; I remember thinking I was glad we were starting with an even number, as it would have been difficult to fire half a person, although technically speaking anyone who worked in this business for very long was half a person already. Then we did a schedule and we figured if we let four people go every month we'd get there. We picked certain dates, trying hard to make it look random so we can say that the word came from on high, or peg it to some client's decision to cut back spending, etc. We pretended with each other in big, long sighs that it was difficult work, very hard, and we would go out afterward and have a nice meal and get shitfaced and take limos home and expense it because of how difficult it was.

Henry had had a pretty interesting life, you might say he had nine lives going until he met me and I guess I capped it at less. He was an actor in his teens, school plays and musicals and so on, and then he went out to Hollywood where he did OK for a while. You can IMDb him. He was in a bunch of films and TV shows and had a few scenes here and there with some name actors. James Spader, for example. But Henry had been born in a trailer park in Florida and so when he got a tiny bit of fame and some money he blew it all up his nose in his twenties. Yeah, he got laid a lot and had a good time but when he started showing up on set high his days were numbered. He just didn't have the sort of juice that would let him behave like that for long, and he had refused one of the producers who had hired him in the hope of sexual dalliance and so his career went away. According to Henry, pretty much every straight male Hollywood star has had to submit to the gay mafia at some point if they wanted to work; I pointed out to him that this kind of talk was homophobic in the extreme and could potentially be a violation of the firm's HR policies, and then we laughed and I bought him a drink.

I learned all this, by the way, the night I took Henry to dinner and made him tell me his life story. He didn't want to drink but I insisted he join me; I told him I thought we should be friends, and I think this came as a shock to him seeing as how he correctly was intuiting that he was on the chopping block.

Anyway, as his story goes, Henry found himself high and dry in LA, with no career, no money, and no friends. Then he met Victoria. Victoria was an ex-model and a nutritionist. She had been down the same road Henry was on and she knew where it led. She had become a junkie and ended up living with an abusive club owner in Miami, getting beaten up regularly, and finally she found the strength to get out. She went to the place where all abused junkie wannabe models go: LA. She got into some kind of all-kale-juice-and-codfish-oil diet thing and supposedly it saved her life. She was studying to become a licensed nutritionist at one of those schools on the second floor of a building on Melrose when she met Henry. She was working at a juice bar and he wandered in drunk, needing to use the bathroom because, after all, he was living in his car at this point. He fell asleep on the toilet and Victoria had to break the door down because they were all afraid that someone had died in there. She found him comatose and called an ambulance and accompanied Henry to the hospital. You can guess the rest. Henry moved in with Victoria to clean himself up and they became lovers. It's a beautiful story, and it almost prompted me to fire him on the spot when I heard it.

Henry's fourth life began when he and Victoria moved to New York so that Henry could pursue his true love, which was art. In New York, Henry and Victoria lived in a fourth-floor walk-up in Brooklyn; Victoria worked in a health food store and tried to set up her nutritionist practice only to discover that people in New York didn't really give a flying fuck about nutrition. And Henry, not coming from a wealthy East Coast or European family with deep ties to people with tons and tons of money, didn't stand a chance in the art world. So, digging down deep and finding a gallant streak he probably didn't know he had, Henry decided to go back to school. He had a pretty good sense of design—his paintings aren't bad, by the way, although they're blurry, the ones I've seen on his website—so he enrolled in one of those graphic design programs at the School of Visual Arts. For two years he studied advertising and he hated it but he knew it was what he had to do.

So Henry miraculously gets a job as a junior art director here at Tate at the really-for-this-business advanced fucking age of thirty-four and he and Victoria start living like human beings. Fourteen years later he's an associate creative director and he's making decent coin, in fact he's pulling in $184K as of the day he was let go. He was actually the go-to guy on the Allstate Insurance account—not thrilling advertising by any means, but he's making the clients happy doing these crappy testimonials. The campaign is doing well in the marketplace, too, but that's not really the point. The point is, Henry was old and he wore pleated Dockers, which I told him not to wear but he did anyway.

The first step in the dance would be to let Henry know in advance that he was in danger of being fired. This was pretty common practice for human resources professionals but I took it to another level. I mean you couldn't exactly go to someone and say "You're going to get the boot in three months no matter what you do" because they might cause all kinds of trouble around the office in the interim, possibly even take legal action against the company, not to mention spreading their negative energy around. And at the same time you don't want to say to them "You're doing a great job you don't have to worry" because then they could claim wrongful termination based on age or something. What you want to do is be considerate, give them a hint that there's a storm coming in, give them a chance to find another job (not likely, but one can always hope) and all at once, and without adieu, give them a swift, unforgiving exit from the shitshow.

So one day as I was standing outside the fish tank (what we called the open-plan creative floor) and was waiting for an elevator, Henry came up and gave me a vaguely Reaganesque nod and earnest smile. At that moment I knew it was time to begin. He said Morning, Eric! or something equally pointless. Normally I would ask him how things were going on Allstate, when was that client presentation again? I mean just to seem interested and to pretend that I was sober or knew or cared what the fuck was going on in my department. And the elevator would come and we would ride together and then when one of us got off I would say Keep me in the loop or something like that, and Henry would get off thinking he had had a worthwhile moment with Mr. Chief Idea Officer. He would probably mention it to the dolts he worked with, saying something like Well Eric and I were talking earlier this morning . . . to make it sound as if he has my ear, we're close, we're like this.

But I just stood there and ignored him. I didn't look up, or rather, I looked up for an instant, enough to let him know that I had heard him but had no interest in replying or engaging with him in any way. He said Morning dude again and I just stared at the wall. I could tell without looking at him that he was momentarily freaked out but immediately pretended to himself that I hadn't heard him even though he knew I had, I guess that's called denial. Then the elevator came and we got on and just stood there like two people who once knew each other but were no longer speaking.

And that was the beginning.

After the elevator incident, Henry started acting predictably tense around me. He would, for example, be the first to arrive at a meeting. I usually tried to arrive fifteen or twenty minutes late for anything. Partly because that was the custom in advertising for the creative people to be late and partly because I was the boss and one way of being the boss was to make everyone wait around for you. So one afternoon as Henry stood lingering outside my office I asked him what he was doing there.

"Aren't we having that Swiffer meeting?" he replied. To which I replied, without looking away from my computer screen, "Are you working on that?"

"Yes, you asked me to chip in on the campaign, you asked me to have some thoughts ready this morning and so I spent the weekend on it," he said in a high-pitched squeal, not wanting to seem confrontational, the raising of one's voice by half an octave or more meant to dissuade the more powerful from attack.

"Well I think there are better uses of one's time than stuffing more shit into that particular shithole," I said with a chummy laugh.

"So I shouldn't stick around for the meeting?" he mumbled, and I said nothing, and I said it without looking at him, pretending to stare at my screen but out of the corner of my eye I could see him there, his body suddenly stiff, him staring at the bare floor with an expression of both confusion and panic.

Yes, I wanted to say to him, this is happening, it is, it's happening now. But I couldn't for legal reasons. And then as if he could read my thoughts, he just walked away.

Post incident I let a couple of weeks slide, to both allow his feelings of terror to stew in him for a while and also to lull him into thinking that the weirdness was maybe over. I had read on the internet that they raise the *toros* in perfect comfort so that when they are first stabbed with the banderilla and begin to bleed and the blood is running into their eyes and there are thousands of people around them screaming but they've never seen more than two or three humans in their lives, these bulls, it just adds to their inability to react appropriately and so they are less of a threat. I had my assistant call Henry in for a meeting. Ten minutes before the meeting was to take place I left the agency and went for a walk. I may have gotten something to eat,

I don't remember. When I got back three hours later my assistant informed me that Henry had been by and he thought we had a meeting and I said, Yeah, I know. The next day I called Henry into my office and this time I didn't leave him hanging. I looked him in the eye and told him he was being taken off the Allstate account. He was stunned. He hadn't seen this coming. Frankly, neither had I, it just came out. He finally asked me Why? and I said something about the client wanting some new blood and how actually I was pleased because this meant Henry was freed up to work on various other assignments.

"What kind of assignments?" he asked me. I said I wasn't sure but that I would think about it and get back to him.

At that point he had to know that he was being fired. But there were still nearly two months left until his end date. For a couple of weeks I just said nothing to him. I'd see him come in and sit in his cubicle and surf the internet and try to look busy. I'd see him go around to the other creative directors and ask them if they needed any help on anything, but everybody knew intuitively that he was going to be let go and they avoided him the way people do in any corporation when they sense someone has lost favor. For weeks no one would make eye contact with him or even say hello to him in the hall. It was if he were literally dying of a contagious disease and so he was being ostracized by those hoping to survive him.

Then one day I had another brainstorm. I called Henry into my office and asked him what he was working on. He tried to cover his shock at the inanity of this question and said he was trying to get on a new business pitch that he had heard was coming down the pike. "So in other words you're not working on anything at the moment," I said with the barest hint of indignation in my voice. He said he was pretty wide open at this point and would love to work on whatever I wanted to toss his way. I let a long silence hang in the room before informing him that it would be difficult for me to justify his salary if he wasn't billing to any client. He sat there, a smiling rictus of fear. I told him that he ought to think about bringing some new business into the agency. Did he have any connections? He said he would think about it. When I had gotten him drunk a few weeks earlier he had spilled to me a couple of interesting facts. One, that he was separated from his wife, and two, that she was living in an apartment on the Upper West Side that had once been owned by a Famous Actor, whom she had briefly dated in LA and had helped through a rough patch.

"What about your wife's nutrition business?" I asked him. Maybe we could do some commercials for her and get her friend to be in them? That would certainly be good for the profile of the agency. Henry agreed wholeheartedly and said he would speak to his ex. Our *danse macabre* was moving along.

So Henry called his ex-wife and told her that he was going to get fired if he didn't come up with something. She agreed to let him pitch the idea of making a few web-based commercials for her consulting practice, which was called Newtritionals, LLC, and she agreed to call her friend about appearing in them. Henry told me that the actor was in Australia filming a movie and couldn't do the spots; I knew that was a lie because I asked one of our casting people to call his agent and find out what his availability was, and they said he was living in Palm Desert and doing nothing at the moment. Nonetheless I'm sure that he had no interest in hawking food supplements on the internet for a girl he banged a few times during a dry spell. But Henry must have really laid it on thick because Victoria pressed Famous Actor, who eventually talked to an old friend of his, a Famous Actress, who played Superman's wife in the '80s. On a rainy night in the fall we got her to show up at a studio on Tenth Avenue. We shot improv until the wee hours and got nothing usable; throughout the ordeal I could see how much pain Henry was in. Then we spent two weeks trying to cut something; I declared the results not worthy of the agency's name, and took Henry to lunch as a way of thanking him for coming through under pressure. And then a few days later I fired him.

It was a beautiful morning. There wasn't a cloud in the sky, and the air had the tiniest hint of a chill in it, the kind of perfect morning that still reminds many New Yorkers of the day the planes flew in. I will never forget the look on his face. He probably thought I wanted to talk to him about the Newtritionals project and maybe what other curiosities we might cook up together. But when he stepped into my office and saw HR Lady there with the beginnings of tears in her eyes, he knew. That's how they all know, by the glistening. He sat in one of the two Eames chairs I had purchased online from the MoMA Design Store and he tried to chuckle as if to say, OK, I get it, and I'm fine with it, but it was obvious that he had been blindsided. Of course in some sense he knew all along but the whole Famous

Actor/Actress incident had no doubt distracted him, as it was meant to do.

I looked at him with my best sad-eyed expression and then there was a pause that could have only lasted a few seconds but seemed much longer. I saw him glance over at a stack of fashion magazines I had put on the floor waiting to be thrown away. I almost had the sense he was counting them, his mind grabbing on to anything to keep it from careening into the abyss. He crossed his legs and looked up at me.

"I'm sorry to say this," I said, nodding with as much earnest emotion as I could muster, "but we're going to have to let you go."

In any good narrative, say a detective story, when at last you know who the killer is, it should be the kind of surprise that you realize was inevitable all along. What Hitchcock called the MacGuffin, what I now suppose I have no choice but to call The Henry. At that point if I were him I would have strangled me to death, but just as the urge to commit an act of senseless violence was rearing up in him—the urge to slap me on the face or smash my Noguchi tabletop with his fist—this is when HR jumps in and tells him about our generous severance package which includes his full salary and health care for nearly five weeks if he agrees to our terms. Realizing he needs the money, Henry just stares at the wall.

"Alright," he says and that was pretty much it. A couple of them have called me a douchebag, one in a voice that was crackling with pain and hatred, he could barely speak he was so angry, he had four children and a fifth on the way, it was tremendously moving. But mostly they're not surprised. The initial clues having been, you know, homeopathic: they're a tiny dollop of the disease, and then the antibodies rush in, and that's the second set of positive clues, and so the subject has a false sense of wellbeing until the bottom drops out. But just as Henry's lips part to speak, to say something else, perhaps a final statement, the two African-American security guards, Damon and Terry, step into my office as if on cue. Henry senses the men behind him, gets up and walks out with them toward the elevators without a word.

It's about 9 AM, I'm being crushed by a hangover and so I'm working out at the health club in my building, trying to sweat it out of my body, all corrupted flesh pixels needing a diagnostic, when a new text pings me. Without breaking stride I fondle my device and see it is from Intern.

> hey!?! wtf!
> so i guess we won't be working together...
> no, wait!!
> change of plans!!!!!
> we WILL be working together!!
> i'm on 8 *cum* c me...........

She's on eight? I can only guess that the editorial company is helping us in-house on something and that's why she's here for the morning? But the tone of her text, very snarky, who does she think she is?

This should be easy. By noon she will be gone.

After concentrating on cardio for five minutes I get a ginger-wheatgrass juice and a green tea infusion and then I head for the showers. The juice girl is incredibly beautiful, she has long skinny arms that look like young birch branches that could wrap around you twice. In the showers, I notice that my cock is a bit harder than it usually is after a workout, I'm feeling pretty horny, I may have mentioned that ever since I began my medications (Adderall, Zoloft, Klonopin, Ativan, occasionally Haldol although I don't always like to admit that) I've had an erection that I can't get rid of no matter what I do. The only comforting thing about this is that I know my boner has nothing to do with Intern, it's just a part of me now, like hair, and no amount of sex or masturbation seems to cure it. For no reason I consider hitting on birch-like juice girl but I fear there is a too-high chance she will say yes.

After my gym time I decide to take the subway to the office just for a change of pace. Usually I call a car service. I live in Brooklyn just off the Williamsburg Bridge, as I may have said earlier, in a loft-like apartment in a brand-new waterfront high-rise called Krave. I usually take a car to work because it's a bit of a hike up Bedford Avenue to the subway and a car is more comfortable and it's also in my contract that I have unlimited use of the Dark Car Corporate limo service. But today I felt like being outside, the weather was nice, which felt like more of an excuse than an actual reason, because I didn't really buy the notion that the weather being nice meant it was a good idea to be outside. It didn't really matter to me one way or the other what the weather was like; if I felt like being outside, or if I had some reason to go outside, then I would generally engineer a way to be out of doors, it was that simple, the weather had little to do with it, except to be able say to myself, when the question arose in my head, "Why are you taking the subway, Eric?" I would have a ready answer and the answer was the niceness of the weather.

Two blocks into my eleven-block walk to the L train I realize why it is that I don't do this very often. A virtual stream of young, fashionable white people, what the savants in our media planning department would refer to demographically as the Creative Class, are rushing toward the train. I don't hate these professionals, since that would be disingenuous, after all I am one of them. I don't really have any opinion about them one way or the other. They are a kind of temporary migration, they are the product of certain economic conditions. About halfway to the subway I am feeling exhausted by the tide I am swimming in and so I need a rest; the night before I had ingested eight or nine saffron-infused apple-ginger absinthe, cognac, and vodka cocktails, the name of which I can't remember, possibly the Caribou Whisperer or the Ragamuffin or the Merkin Sniffer and I'm still feeling somewhat ill. I pop into a coffee place called Silhouette that is frequented for some reason by mixed-race French people from Paris who are living in Brooklyn because the dollar makes it cheap for them, and I order a scat coffee for twenty-six dollars and a bowl of fresh berries for twelve dollars.

I'm not in the least bit hungry but somehow the idea of fresh berries seems like a good one, like a smart idea, a smart way to start my morning, even though my morning began hours ago at some sleepless and unremarked moment between night and day. The scat coffee comes first and I take a sip and wonder if it isn't just burnt Maxwell House. Then a bowl of fresh, locally grown berries arrives and the moment I see them I know I will not be eating them. I sit and look out the window at the pretty little fishies darting up and down the stream on their way to their exciting jobs in the worlds of fashion and art and reality TV and suddenly I don't feel well. What is it? I ask myself, and I respond by saying "I don't know, Eric," out loud. "I don't know what it is."

And I don't. I've been diagnosed before with certain somewhat common illnesses, most of them mental in nature, but that doesn't explain why I haven't eaten in almost three days, since the time I met her.

On the sidewalk outside a young woman in a Ted Lapidus jacket and carrying a Stella by Stella McCartney by Stella M for Talentless by Rich Daddy bag is tying her shih tzu to someone's bicycle, and now the owner of the bike is coming up to her and saying, like, um, that's my bike? And this woman is saying she's just getting a Clover-press coffee to go and she'll be back in four-point-two minutes, she promises, and suddenly I'm having a full-blown panic attack: the desire to jump in front of a bus is so strong in me I grip my chair and sit there, rigid, and hope it stops. This has happened before so I know what to do, only I don't have any Klonopin in my Crumpler shoulder bag. After about an hour I decide I'm not going into work today. After another hour I realize I'm not doing anything today. I am aware that I am having one of my episodes, since as I've said I've had them before, and they always do pass eventually, although this one seems a bit more persistent than the others. My phone has been ringing and buzzing from time to time because I have some important meetings, in fact I was supposed to meet with HR Lady and let two more copywriters go today, and no one knows what has happened to me, I can just imagine the concern growing with each voice mail. But I have the sudden and I realize nonsensical thought that if I answer my mobile device or even check my messages something terrible will happen to me, that all manner of doom will be unleashed upon me, from financial ruin to torture and death, which I am fully aware is silly. There is also the text from Intern that I would rather not see, even to delete it, which may be contributing to my unalterable inability to deal with my unreality.

At this point the patchouli-scented half-Senegalese woman from behind the counter comes up and asks if there's anything wrong with my fresh berries because I haven't touched them and I say, no, they're absolutely delicious, I just changed my mind, I'm so sorry. I almost add that if I were to leave this place I may run headlong into a truck just to stop it from going on any longer. What from going on any longer? I don't know, all of it. I want to laugh, and for a brief moment I do. Some people look at me and then they ignore me. After another half hour the episode subsides and I am able to get up and walk back home and play Halo for a few hours. Then I go to sleep without checking my e-mail or returning any calls. It occurs to me that maybe I'm a) experiencing some unexplained resistance to sacking the two copywriters I was supposed to have sacked today, and b) I am semi-falling in love with her, the girl whose name I don't know, or care to know, which is impossible, but I can deal with all that when the fires die down.

After a good many hours of lying there trying to sleep I finally give up at 5:45 AM and instead of going to the gym I decide to check my mail and deal with what inevitably will be the crisis of my not showing up yesterday. I am surprised to discover only two e-mails from my assistant, the first one inquiring about my travel plans for an upcoming commercial shoot in Los Angeles, California, and the second one, from about midmorning, inquiring as to my whereabouts.

"(HR Lady) was just wondering where she might locate you, Eric, she left a couple of messages, will reschedule a check-in for this afternoon?" was my assistant's query. I checked my voice mail, and there were also two, both from HR Lady herself as had been expected, both polite and professional, and both employing the verbs "touch base" and "loop back." What this means is it is not even 6 AM and I've already decided not to go to the gym, a plan I could easily change, as I really don't have to be into the office for four hours, but I find it hard to rearrange a plan once it has been commenced, and besides, yesterday's panic attack had occurred not long after going to the gym, so maybe it is a good idea to not repeat myself. The only problem is what to do with the intervening hours before I am due in the office. I could go online and search for other gyms in the area, I could just join a new one, but that seems a bit excessive. Time passes. I look out the east-facing windows at the sky, pinkish like plated salmon croquettes, and blueish like, I suppose, deskulled brains, cold enough to see steamy smoke, or was it smoky steam, rising from the oil furnaces in the three flats that lie between me and the bridge. I call and order delivery of two almond-soymilk lattes from Marlow & Sons, and then I call Silhouette, the Franco-Senegalese-Brazilian café, and try to order a bowl of fresh berries again but they don't deliver. I hang up and look around my flat, thinking about getting some furniture one of these days and then I wait for my beverages. Waiting, I realize, isn't the time between things, it's the thing itself.

When the lattes finally do arrive ($14) they are less than piping hot and I refuse them, though I do pay for them and tip the guy twenty dollars for his trouble (total $34). Three and a half hours later, at the Tate headquarters in midtown, HR Lady is waiting for me in the holding area outside my office. Her name is Helen, she is not married, reputed to have a long-time boyfriend who she never speaks about, lives alone, and enjoys foreign films and getting outside the city on weekends, according to her Match.com profile, which I looked up once. She is feigning concern about my health, wondering if I am alright.

"Are you alright?" she asks, adding, without meaning it in the slightest, "We were worried about you!"

"I haven't had my Starbucks if that's what you mean." HR Lady uses "Starbucks" to mean coffee so around her I do too.

"I'm talking about yesterday!"

"Didn't you get my text?" I lied.

"No," she lied, pretending she didn't know I was lying.

"Oh they musn't have gone through. Fucking AT&T!" I thought it would be interesting to push the lie a little further and see if HR Lady would go along with it to the bitter end. "I was surprised I didn't hear from you so I sent the same text again and I left you a voice mail? I think I left you two voice mails, in fact, I'm so sorry you didn't get them, shit, Jesus, I don't know what's going on around here anymore."

"Me neither," she says, wondering what I was up to. "I didn't get any of them. Did you send them from your iPhone or your BlackBerry? It's T-Mobile, right?" For a moment I thought she meant it, that she didn't know I was only toying with her. But she kept it up so I knew she was just playing along. "You know how telcom is around here ever since Kyle was let go," she says with a shrug and a smile and a little wave of her hands, or is it a rolling of her eyes and a look of minory contempt? I can't quite tell. I don't say anything.

"Shall we do it now?" she then asks. And I say "Sure! Let's do it! Let's get it over with!" And then, "Ugh, what a life!" to which she says "Here we go!" with mock-ironic morbidness. Then she asks my assistant to call the copywriters, Dave and Bill.

Meanwhile I have mail, the usual stack of bubble-wrapped DVDs from production houses touting shitty directors—"Peter Rossi Shoots Kids!" as if that's either funny or original—and I throw them all away immediately without even considering watching a single second of this crap. There is also an inter-office envelope which feels empty. I am about to open it when Dave and Bill arrive and see HR Lady there and immediately they know.

"I guess this is it," one of them says with a forced chuckle. They always say that, to soften the humiliation, to own it, they always chuckle, as well they should. But I'm not concerned with Dave and Bill right now because I am too pissed off at the stupidity of my assistant who called both of them in at the same time. The rules of this are, according to the lawyers, that we can only fire one at a time, unless they are a team, and Dave and Bill are both copywriters and thus not a team. Meaning one of them, either Dave or Bill, we haven't determined the order yet, is going to have to stand there while the other one gets the news in private. It's humiliating, but on the other hand, the gyrations that I've put both of them through in the past few months were much more intense.

Dave, for example, is forty-six and his wife just had a child not more than two weeks ago. Disgusting, ugly little knot of fat, frightening really, and when I first saw the picture he e-mailed to the department I thought perhaps the child was a bird-headed dwarf, which sounds like something I made up but actually that's a real medical term for a kind of mutation, or birth defect, related to but not entirely the same as being a pinhead. So I had my assistant, I suppose I should include her name here at some point, it's Cheryl, or Cherie, and she is not as attractive as I'd hoped for, but it's too late to say anything, I had Cheryl or Cherie send Dave and his wife a cute onesie and a bottle of champagne and a warm note from me personally. This could, of course, be interpreted in a number of ways, that it was part of my slow turning of the spit that Dave was curing on, since I had begun dropping hints that he was getting the boot months ago, or that I was gifting him out of guilt at what I knew was his fate. Bill, on the other hand, was single and homosexual, although he doesn't admit this publicly, but no one whose shirt is that perfectly pressed and shrink-wrapped into his trousers could possibly be straight with the exception of myself. I had called Bill into my office around the same time I was dropping hints with Dave, and I told Bill he was going to get a big promotion and a sizable raise, I just had to get approval from the holding company. Every so often he would ask how that was going and I would tell him they had a salary freeze or something but not to worry. Since we had decided long ago to fire both of them on the same day I thought it would be an interesting juxtaposition to compare their reactions back to back. I mean this whole business is pure evil, why sugarcoat it? In fact, why not broadcast it?

When we finish terminating them, Damon and Terry stand hulkingly by the elevators with them, waiting to take their ride of shame down to the street, and HR Lady asks me if I want to go to lunch because there is something we need to discuss.

"I'm not hungry," I say, thinking that it is strange I have no appetite since I haven't eaten anything for three-point-five days now.

"What is it?"

She gets up and closes the door while I open the interoffice envelope in my hand. She immediately begins to talk about this new intern in the production department on eight when I pull a single sheet of paper from the envelope and look at it.

> *What's a girl to do? Well, the sensible thing is to disappear. But some girls are not so sensible, are they? Some grrrls get so drunk they can't remember things & then they get kicked out of the lair (so maddeningly rude & annoyingly kewt all at once) & then they try to stay in touch but that doesn't work & then—life is strange & beautiful all at once is it not?—they go & get a new internship—where?—OMG what a coincidence!!!!*

The printout is not signed. As I read it HR Lady is asking me if I have anything to say. "About what?" I ask. Then she says they didn't know that the girl and I had a relationship prior to us taking her on as a production intern, and if they had they wouldn't've hired her, but on her first day, which was yesterday, she comes to HR Lady and says she needs to divulge something of a personal nature for reasons of personal integrity, honesty, due diligence, and all around professionalism.

"A prior relationship?" I say as if I don't know what the words mean.

"Yes."

"A prior relationship with who?"

"With you."

"She said she had a prior relationship with me? Like what did she mean by that?"

"Well she didn't elaborate but I understood it to mean you had had some kind of . . ." And then she hesitates before sing-songing the word "liaison" in a lurid key.

I sit there for a few moments and consider my options. I had guessed she was capable of pulling some kind of stunt like this, and I had planned on getting rid of her anyway (can you fire someone who isn't getting paid? I think you can) but she had trumped me, now it would be impossible to remove her because it would look like retribution, but if I had been able to fire her before she said anything about it, and then she said it after the fact, that would look like revenge on her part. Meanwhile I could lie and say nothing had ever happened between us, and everyone would believe me, or at least they would believe I had the upper hand, which would amount to the same thing. Besides, it was true, pretty much nothing had happened. All this to say: she is a smart girl.

"She was working at Unkindest Cuts, which is where I met her, and then I ran into her at a bar in Bushwick and she picked me up," I say, leaving out the part where I asked her to go into the bathroom and do some coke with me and bought her round after round of Cîrocs and then a bottle of prosecco and poured her, as the expression goes, into a cab and peeled her shirt away when we got into my place where we made out before she barfed on my floor.

"And that's the extent of it. I don't even remember her name."

"Seriously?" HR Lady says, with an expression that contained both contempt for my womanizing and, of course, admiration for it. "You don't remember her name?"

"Is it Sarah? Saree? Marilyn? Something like that."

"Didn't you know how old she was?" HR asks. I don't even honor the question with a look of feigned lack of understanding. Then HR Lady tells me that there's nothing they can do but fulfill her internship for the summer and that I should perhaps just steer clear of the eighth floor for a while? OK, sure fine. But then:

"What did she say about me?"

"What do you mean what did she say about you?" HR says.

"I mean did she say she, like, had a thing for me?"

"No. Why? Are you saying she's into you? Or, wait, you like her, is that it?"

I don't bother to answer her, I just say "I'll stay off eight. Promise you. Won't ever step off the lift." The less HR Lady knows about my theories regarding the dangers of this particular girl, the better. She nods, our business finished for today. But she doesn't get up. She sighs and gives me a look. Is this her "Eric you should know better than to sleep with nineteen-year-olds" look, or is it her "Eric why are you wasting your time with nineteen-year-old girls when there are full-fledged women available to you, living breathing *women* sitting right in front of you" look? Or is it her "Fuck, dude, you are the Man" look? I don't know and I don't ask. She is making me extremely uncomfortable so I pretend to get an e-mail in my phone and I swipe at it and ignore her.

"They'll be OK" she finally says, making it clear she is talking about something else. "Won't they?"

"Who?"

"Dave and Bill?"

"Gee, I hope so," I say, meaning it, meaning: wanting her to know I mean it. "They're really good guys. They'll land on their feet."

She gives me another one of those looks. "Sometimes I wonder."

"You wonder if they're good guys? They're awesome guys!" I say. I know that's not what she was wondering about but I just don't want to go down any kind of quasi-moralizing or regret or second-thoughts path or anything like that with her.

"No, I mean I wonder sometimes about what we're doing. About, you know, all the pain we're causing. Do you believe in karma?"

The moment she says the word I picture her going all Namaste, up near the front of the yoga class, with her prayer hands, trying to get the eye of a male instructor, the one ten years younger and with a topknot. A topknot on a guy is like a sign on his forehead saying "I'll go down on you for a really long time and make it seem totally unselfish but really I'm kind of worried that I'm gay." So I try to look at her as if she is being overly sensitive, I get that, and I appreciate it, but.

"We're ensuring the survival of the agency," I say, repeating the rote justification speech that she herself handed me when we started this whole firing thing months ago. "Over four hundred people work here and if we don't cut back significantly due to the ongoing economic situation they'll all be out on the street, every one of them."

She sighs again and gives me that look, which I now interpret as a look of pride mixed with shame, pride at her power in this whole thing, pride at being entrusted with so much responsibility, but all of it mitigated by pride's shadow side. That's a human being for you. I had neither pride nor shame in what we were doing. It was just my job. I was saving the agency and conducting a thought experiment at the same time, one that could have far-reaching implications for corporate culture. I had carefully and painstakingly created a very specific milieu, a culture of fear and paranoia, and we were watching it unfurl and grow, like something in a large and fetid petri dish, our own Milgramesque biosphere of doom. I suppose one might be justified in being proud of such a creation but that would be self-serving, and shame equally so; I was doing it for larger reasons, and I was giving it away like you would a vaccine that saves millions of lives.

She still sits there and doesn't move, or won't. I want her out of my office. If I am being completely honest I would say her body language means she wants me to hold her and cuddle her and tell her everything is going to be fine. A week ago I might have entertained the thought of such things, cuddling or at least making out, but I feel nothing for HR Lady today, not a shred of interest even as she crosses her legs and fails to readjust her skirt. They really are great legs, and it isn't that she's unattractive, as I have said, it's just that for the past several days, whenever I catch a glimpse of a thigh or a breast the only thing I can think of is Intern's fecund, glowing lips, her shining eyes, her breasts. It's driving me nuts and I don't know what to do about it but jerk off into the trash basket for the second time today, only I can't do that at the moment without a certain degree of embarrassment because there's someone in my office.

When she finally leaves (was that a backward angry jealous glance she gave me on the way out? yes) I check my stocks as a means of killing a few minutes and then I go up to eight.

The eighth floor houses our production department. At any given time, the New York office of Tate Worldwide (New York being the largest of our fifty-six offices around the world) will be in the midst of producing eight or ten commercials for our various clients. The way advertising works is simple: we charge huge companies millions and millions of dollars a year to come up with the big ideas that will help them to grow their businesses, to define for themselves an expandable niche in their market, to give them something to stand on, a mission to purport, a flag to wave. Ad agencies exist for the same reason that mercenaries do. An oil company can't be in the business of, say, executing the popular leader of a left-wing opposition group in some Central American democracy, that just isn't a job description that they can put up on their LinkedIn page. So they have to hire a consultant who hires a global risk-management firm who hires a mercenary unit who hires a local criminal gang to get the job done. It's the same with what we do. XXX Pharmaceuticals wants to believe that it is in the business of making the world a better place, not of convincing people to take overpriced drugs they don't need (and that can't be proven to be much more effective than a placebo). So they outsource their lying to us. We then pretend to help them make the world a better place. All we really do is enable their fantasies about themselves by holding their hand through the difficult years-long process of bringing a drug to market. In the course of that, it's our job to pretend to be coming up with ideas when really all we are doing is taking the ideas that they have already given us in their PowerPoint documents and making them look like they were ours in the first place and therefore worth the many millions they are paying us. It's useless but in the end what human endeavor isn't? We have meeting after meeting and write draft after draft of a single fifteen-second commercial, exposing these scripts to real people to get their feedback, in what is known as qualitative or "qual" testing, before gauging the spot's real-world CPI—Consumer Persuasion Index—in quantitative or "quant" testing, in which each commercial is assigned a numerical value supposedly indicating its true effectiveness, the entire process meant to ultimately determine whether it would be more effective to frighten people into buying a drug because without it their children might die or frightening them into buying a drug because if they don't their peers will ostracize them for being terrible parents. Once real moms and dads have signed off on our concept, we hand these so-called ideas to a director and a production company and ask them to "add value," which means, "Can you try to take this mind-numbingly boring piece of machine-made bullshit and force-fit a modicum of humanity into it?" Normally this is done via casting, trying to find human-looking people to stand in front of the camera and smile and give the thumbs-up to life. That usually works. Then when the commercial is finished, we celebrate ourselves and our achievements at an awards banquet from which we take home prizes in categories such as "Best Editing for a Fifteen-Second Unbranded Direct-to-Consumer Web-Based Pharmaceutical Campaign" and so on.

I always get confused on the eighth floor. When you get off the elevators you can go one of two ways: toward the bathrooms or toward the receptionist. Having made that decision you can then go either right or left, ultimately giving you the option of the four compass directions. I can never remember where anyone's office is and so I always end up just walking around the perimeter of the building until I find who I am looking for. Today I get off the elevators and decide to go toward the receptionist, who is on her break apparently, as there's a temp sitting in her spot and he looks like a young Paul Rudd with facial hair, obviously an actor who doesn't have a trust fund; i.e., hopeless. From the receptionist's desk I randomly choose left, and I walk toward the Twenty-ninth Street side of the building. When I get to the row of offices that rings the floor I randomly choose to turn right and I start walking. Everyone sees me and looks up from their desks and waves or grins; this isn't something they would do for anyone who walked down the hall, but one of the consequences of creating a dynamic of fear is a high degree of sycophancy resulting in a good deal of performative smiling. Our poor wannabe-actor temp thinks that by sitting there stone-faced and not participating in these corporate rituals he will save his soul; what he doesn't understand is that all of the phoniness required of his soulless peers takes far more acting skill, courage, and devotion to craft than he will ever see on any not-for-profit stage in his entire life.

If asked I will say I am looking for Tom Bridge, but I happen to know that Tom is in Prague shooting a series of spots for a tire company. I get to the corner of the building and turn right (the only way I can go unless I want to retrace my steps) and then I see Tom's assistant, a hipster clown named Jake. I call him a clown because he is one; he works on weekends at a children's hospital in Westchester. Apparently he was a drug addict and then he became a clown as a part of his recovery program; we even honored him with our Actually Good Person We Mean It of the Month Award.

Jake the Clown sees me walking toward him and says, "Are you looking for Tom?" I don't know if I should lie and say yes since that is the ostensible reason I've come to this floor in the first place or if I should lie and say no since that's the truth but it means I must have another reason for being here and that one I don't want to divulge.

"Isn't he in Prague?" I say, splitting the difference.

"He was supposed to leave last night but his flight got canceled can you believe that it was a nightmare he's leaving in an hour do you want to see him I can maybe squeeze you in just kidding." I'm staring at Clown, who's in full '80s mode today, parachute pants and one of those Palestinian scarves and a Members Only warm-up jacket, and I'm wondering what his getup is, does he put on a big pink wig and a red nose and paint his face white, or does he know he already looks enough like a clown to make a sick child laugh? Just then Tom's voice is heard from inside his office.

"Eric!" he is yelling. "Eric you douchebag come in here don't go away I need to talk to you before my car comes!" I go into Tom's office. He is sitting amid a pile of DVD reels that is almost as large as he is, which is considerable.

"Yo, asshole," I greet him, closing the door, "why aren't you getting your knob sucked by a Czech hooker right now?" This is how Tom and I talk to each other; the day I learned that I would have to terminate him in Q2 of the next fiscal I considered not being so buddy-buddy with him, then I changed my mind. "Close the door," he says, even though I already have. He tosses a DVD of work from an animation company called Phawg into the trash basket and takes his earphones off. "Did you say something?"

"No," I say. The sounds of a live Rush concert are coming from his iPhone. Rush is Tom's favorite band; he turns off the trollish sounds and looks up at me.

"I can't believe you fucked her," he says.

"Fucked who, your wife?" I say. "Ha ha just kidding, in case you were wondering."

"Funny," he says. "I'm talking about that very hot girl we just hired."

"First of all, she may be funny and smart and all but she's insane," I inform him, "so you might want to stay away from her entirely, or find a way to fire her before I do. And second of all, I didn't have sex with her."

"Which is not what she's telling everyone."

"Oh bullshit she's a drug addict," I say.

"So are you," he says.

"Have a nice trip, dickhead," I say to him as I open the door and head out, turning back to ask him what he's doing with the DVD cases. He says he doesn't know he just felt like saving them.

"See you in lala," he is saying as I leave.

"What?"

"I'm flying directly from Prague to LA for the FreshIt thing. I'll be there for callbacks."

"Cool," I say, "that's awesome, but I'm not going to that shoot."

"No?" he says. "I thought you were."

"Why would I waste my time with that shit?" I say.

"Because the account is in trouble."

"Not my problem," I say. Then as I am closing his door he says, "By the way, she's uploading some spots to the FTP, I'd try the dub room. I mean, assuming you want to find her."

"I don't, actually," I lie. "I want her out of here by EOD."

"Right," he says. "Will do."

I walk out of his office and down the hall I hadn't walked down before, hoping for a random encounter rather than having to actually set foot in the dub room which would be too obvious. I end up circling the floor two times but I don't see her.

I probably would have kept doing it all afternoon except my phone rings and it's Seth Krallman, my old friend whom I hate.

"What up, gangsta?" I say into my phone as I head toward the elevator. "Why'd you stand me up the other night, dog?" One of the reasons I hate Seth Krallman is because he talks like he's from the ghetto when actually he is from Greenwich, Connecticut, and I tend to talk that way when I'm with him just to mask the fact I dislike him so intensely. I've hated Seth Krallman ever since he got clean and became a yoga teacher and changed his name to Hanuman or Ganesh or something. No, the truth is I always hated him; we shared a big house together at Brown and he thinks this means we have some kind of Special Bond. He's a pretentious idiot, a so-called avant garde playwright who had twelve or thirteen seconds of notoriety in the East Village in the late '90s when he chained himself to the stage of a tiny theater for a month as some kind of protest slash performance, peeing in a crystal bowl and mixing it with champagne and drinking it every night at precisely midnight, while reciting some poetry. I avoided him for years but he friended me recently and keeps wanting us to hang out, I'm pretty sure that he's gearing up to ask me for a job. He comes from a rich family, as I alluded, but his father invested badly and lost most everything in '08 so Seth's monthly automatic deposit has dwindled away—he has to work now to pay his rent and his medical bills, because he is bipolar, and without his meds and his therapy the man is useless. So he wants to invite me to this really cool opening and after-party in the 'wick and maybe, I'm guessing, that's when he'll ask me if I can help him get into advertising. I have nothing to do tonight and need to take my mind off myself and maybe talk to people so I say yes. Then I immediately regret it but he doesn't know that yet. So he starts to ask me how work is going and I pretend that the elevator is killing my reception even though I am not in the elevator.

I get to the opening before Seth does. It's at a storefront gallery on an industrial section of Johnson Avenue; the space used to be a skateboard shop and now it's rented out by the three guys who started *Rodney* magazine, and they show art in it. *Rodney* is considered the epicenter of cool in Bushwick right now and since Bushwick is the epicenter of cool in New York that makes *Rodney* the most boring thing on the planet. Normally the thought of the Fucking *Rodney* Scene would send me into an uncontrollable rage and thus I would avoid it entirely, but I am here to see the hateful ex-junkie yoga master and hang out with him and listen to him go on about how avant garde theater is dead, seriously, it's a tragedy, I mean Heiner Müller wouldn't even get his work seen today. His shtick is really one of the saddest things ever and maybe that's why he cheers me up so easily.

The art space is packed and the kids are spreading out into the street like a fungus. Never before have I seen so many people in one place who are exactly the same: the same age, the same race, the same wardrobe, the same facial hair, the same taste in music, socioeconomic background, college experience, shoes, political beliefs, and hair; but I suppose what really unites them is the shared fantasy that they are rebels, subversively unique individuals creating their own style for themselves.

I make a quick spin through the crowd and can't find Vishnu. He's always late anyway, it's one of the many things I can't stand about him. I squeeze inside the storefront past a girl wearing a Shepard Fairey Obama Hope T-shirt in which she's sliced his eyes out, showing her nipples through his empty eye sockets, and I can't tell if she means this ironically or if she means anything by it at all, maybe her nipples doubling as the POTUS's eyes is just a coincidence. I then get it, I make a connection to the concept behind the art show, which is called "Show Us Your Tits!" and it features lots of photos (taken, it seems, by anyone who can push the button on a camera) of girls flashing their breasts in bars, at parties, on the street, and so on, the pinnacle of art world cool reappropriating bad TV from over a decade ago, and with unicorns.

All in all it's a pretty good show. A lot of the pictures are so lo-res they look like they were screen-grabbed off YouTube or at best shot on old phones. The whole thing must have taken at least an entire Saturday to curate and hang, affixed to the wall as it all is with duct tape; perhaps it took the whole weekend if there was any marijuana in play. The truth is I've never liked art very much, and I can't decide if I like this show because it's not really art at all, it's just stupid, or if maybe I hate this shit because it's trying so hard not to be art and there's nothing more arty than that. I try to think of another profession in which people do something all the while claiming they aren't. Would a doctor do that? Anyway, I begin to feel sick to my stomach so I go to the one makeshift bathroom at the back of the space but there's a long line of drunk girls and so I head back outside for some so-called air.

That's when I see Gandhi talking to two black guys in the middle of the street, and not the kind of white black guys you normally see at these sorts of things, the kind of white black guys who can stomach us like the white black guys in the band TV on the Radio seem to be able to. No, these were actual black guys, they really stood out, they did not even have semi-ironic Afro picks in semi-ironic 'fros and they did not call each other "Negro" or wear bow ties or read James Baldwin on the subway. Seth introduces them to me as P-Mouse and Grain or something like that, it's hard for me to hear because a faux–hair metal band is playing out of the back of a Budget rental truck parked on the street.

"Hey, did you guys see the art? What do you think?" I ask. Titmouse and Plain are in the music business, Seth is telling me, and they don't give a shit about art.

"We don't give a shit about art," D-Louse says. "It's stupid." He then says he doesn't think this crap here is art anyway, it's just some bad pictures of some like dumbass rich girls flashing some of their rich-ass skin. I start to say something about the art being about a subversive, if not downright gangsta, appropriation by the highbrow culture establishment of a lowbrow pop icon, and Plane says "Who gives a fuck?" which kind of makes me want to hug him. Then Seth says these two guys wanted to meet me because they have just started a music production company, they've been producing some tracks out of the back blocks of Crown Heights, they are going to blow up any second, and, wait for it, they were thinking of getting into commercials. I could, see, get in on the ground floor, get a good deal on some demos before they were snatched up by the likes of Nike and Diesel.

Ten minutes later we are sitting at a rusty metal table in the back of a place called Midnight Drab on DeKalb Avenue. It has no sign and not even much of a door and nobody is even sure if Midnight Drab is really the name of it, it's just what the place is called, at least by Seth. The blacks are ordering gin and juice and so I order one, too. I'd already had the better part of a bottle of red wine at my apartment before coming to the art show, and for a moment I fear the dangerous combination of grape and juniper, as it's not something I've experimented with before, but we'll see. An hour later the conversation turns to all these great commercials that people have been seeing on ESPN, the one where the guy runs up the side of a building and explodes, the one where the car comes out the guy's ass, I have no idea what they're talking about. But as I am thinking about excusing myself and going home to masturbate to the pictures in some French fashion rag, B-Louse, or is it Painboy, unfurls a one-hit bumper in his enormous hand. Alright, maybe I'll stay for another G&J, even if it does mean enduring the kings of alt-garage hip-hop pressing on me their sampler CDs. I grab the bumper and lean down under the table and pretend I dropped something and do a hit; when I arise the guys are chuckling while Ravi Shankar makes some kind of face.

"No worries, I bought it from the bartender," says Louse, meaning it's all good here. I do another hit, left nostril this time, without attempting to disguise it. Seth gives me a micro-look like, That's cool, you do your thing, and I can be here with you, because I'm a superior being now, I've reached this higher yogic plane of sobriety, I am but a mute witness to the fog of human sadness here before me. I try to hand the vial to Seth as a joke and he waves it off, not getting me. But to my surprise, Louse and Jane wave it off, too.

"All you, dog."

So now I'm drunk and high and sitting with three idiots, guys who finish sentences with "dog" or "yo" or "fag"; unfortunately this constitutes the most satisfying social event of my week, not including the sexual encounter of four-point-five days ago.

We decide to leave and go to the after-party for the opening, which is at a loft in Ridgewood. Seth still has the Range Rover that his parents bought him as a birthday present back when they were flush, and he hasn't sold it yet even though he can't afford the upkeep; I think he may have said something about the insurance having lapsed and what a pain in the ass alternate-side parking is. After we are at the loft party for a few minutes, which is packed with the same people who were at the opening, and our hip-hop friends are still the only African-Americans in the crowd, some guy with a waxed mustache and an eye patch comes around holding a bucket collecting money to pay for the keg of Milwaukee's Best that is already gone and that's when I realize I made a mistake in coming out tonight at all. Seth and the guys are talking to a couple of young girls; Seth thinks he is getting somewhere with them because of how Street his friends are, and how this confers status on him, but really the girls are not paying attention to him, they're just thinking about the possibility of hooking up with Louse or Pain for the tweet of it.

I take out my phone to call the car service to come pick me up when I see there's a text I didn't know I had.

turn arownd !!!

Fuck.

I make a point of not looking around the room, I just stuff my phone back in my jacket pocket and watch Seth and the girls and black guys standing in a little circle. One of the girls is wearing a diagonal-striped Diane von Furstenberg dress from the '80s. She has the wrong body type for it, but she doesn't seem to care. In my mind I'm just getting into this heavy critique of her because I don't want to look around and let Intern think I am looking for her. After a minute or two I realize I forgot to call the car service, but that will entail taking my phone out again, which Intern, if she is indeed watching me from somewhere in the big crumbling warehouse of poseurs, will interpret as my caring.

Then I see Titmouse offer a bump to the girls and they enthusiastically buy in. So the skinny young white chicks from the suburbs go off with the guys from Crown Heights, stepping on a radiator and climbing out a window and onto a roof where they will do the coke, with one of the girls giving an OMG look to a friend of hers standing by the refrigerator as she takes the enormous hand of T-Louse, and the friend is trying to take their picture with her phone but she is too late, she missed it, they are outside now.

I look back to Seth, and he's staring at his phone as a means of avoiding the pain of rejection that is nonetheless etched into his face. Perhaps he's thinking that if he still did drugs he would be getting some sex tonight, possibly in the front of his awesome Range Rover where he parked it around the corner on Onderdonk. Or perhaps he's thinking what I would be thinking, which is that Pitmouse and Brain have betrayed him, left him hanging there, and even though they barely know each other, it was a pretty thoughtless move. But no, it wasn't that, it was just a numbers thing, there were two cute girls, and three horny guys, and the girls had probably just moved here from college, from Bard or Reed or one of those other places where rich people send their kids so they can learn how to spot the latent sexism and racism inherent in contemporary culture, especially advertising, and now their degree qualifies them to make art about the latent sexism and racism inherent in contemporary culture, especially advertising, and for a few years they do this, until they realize how stupid it all is, and then they decide to go and actually work in advertising instead of critiquing it, to spend some time "in the belly of the beast" as it were, and maybe one day make art or write a graphic novel about *that*, which they never do.

I am looking around for something to drink, not that I need it, and I haven't eaten anything in almost five days which is only exacerbating my quasi-dystopic mood, but every red plastic cup is empty except for the ones with cigarette butts in them.

Seth finally looks up from his phone and scans the room. I assume he's looking for me, or at least someone else he can glom on to. At the moment I turn away from him and squeeze out the four-foot-round punched-out hole in the drywall that leads to the back stairs, I can tell he saw me and that he could see that I saw him and pretended I did not.

I keep going and I don't stop or look back until I am down at the street. If I heard his steps behind me or his voice calling out to me I would probably just tell him what an asshole he is, how I can't stand his goddam month-long theater wanks, they are pure torture, go keep bees on your own time, don't charge people to watch you learn Farsi, and he needs to wake up and sell his car because I am not going to get him a job.

Once out on Onderdonk I decide to walk past the projects to Marcy because sometimes you can get lucky and find a cab there. For a second I'm self-concious about walking past the PJs with my phone to my ear as I've heard that there's been a lot of iPhone jackings recently, a slew of girls have been getting punched in the face while talking on their mobile devices at all hours of the day and night, it serves them right, in a way, it's not even about the phone it's about the obliviousness, there,

here's your phone back, lady. I'm just trying to keep my mind occupied so that I'm not scared or don't go nuts when I hear my name said aloud. I'm not being mugged, muggers don't know my name and besides the voice is a girl's.

I spin around and it's her across the street, coming toward me. She's wearing a skirt that hugs her thighs and those Hunter boots. Also a gray hoodie that I think says Tribecastan across the front and a floppy hat that I'm guessing was knitted by those French grandmothers on that website that was super cool a few years ago. It wasn't really cold enough for such a hat but I could not deny that it framed her face well, with one of the earflaps slightly more askew than the other. As a rule I refuse to watch any film made after 1936 but occasionally I will make an exception for the French director Jean-Luc Godard, and Intern looks very much like a 'shopped version of Chantal Goya, she has the same bangs and the same kind of eyes and features, large lips and high cheekbones, and she has none of Goya's sad, little-girl winsomeness, and she does not have Goya's bright, brittle, optimistic smile, either, and she's young, as I have said before, but exactly how young I don't know. And her smile does have a kind of odd glaze, a rare color mixed from mischief, neediness, intimidating intelligence, ironic adolescent stupidness, beauty, and so on.

"Hey, Eric!" neo-Chantal is saying. I still don't know her real name.

"Hey."

She gets to my side of the street and just stands there waiting for me to do something like walk away. I would but even that would be a form of communication and I desperately do not want to engage in any kind of dialog with her. She tilts her head to the side and there's the smile and a little laugh as if to say, "We hooked up, sort of, you and I, and then you ignored me but I'm fiendish and fierce and I got a job at your company and now you have to be my friend, too bad for you, and we'll hook up again one of these days, but probably not tonight?"

I hang on that thought for a beat too long and then she says, "What did you think of the party?"

I decide to pretend that I never got her text. "What party? This party? Were you there?"

"I know you got my text, Eric, I saw you reading it!" And she laughs again, does the smile thing again, and I look away.

"OK, cool beans, I got your text." I don't know what else to say. At this point I can't tell if my fear of her is what's making me nauseous or if it's something else, possibly the smell of burning plastic coming from under the street, an electrical fire or something.

"Are you mad at me?"

"Why would I be mad at you?"

"Well maybe because I got an internship at your agency without even asking you about it or anything? Also about puking on your imported throw rug."

The girl can be funny; I can't help but laugh.

"Ah, I knew there was a human person in there somewhere," she says with a slanted little wink. I should say this is disarming because it is disarming.

"It's a free planet you can say whatever it is you want to say to whomever it is you want to say it." Even as I speak the line I know it is incredibly lame, even the construction of the sentence, the useless repitition of "it is," the overly correct use of "whomever." I am drunk and doomed all at once.

"You *are* mad. Ohhhh! Goody!"

"No, I'm not angry, why would I be angry at you?"

"Because I'm stalking you??!?"

"*Are* you stalking me?"

"Isn't it obvious?" she says with a laugh as if stalking some-one were pretty much the same thing as saying hi to them. She is so weird I have to look away again, and then I think of that French phrase, *jolie laide*, "beautiful ugly," and then for some-thing better to do I'm reading the badly painted signage on a warehouse, it says USED POLICE CARS UNLIMITED, THE NAME SAYS IT ALL™, which has to be the worst tagline of all time.

"To be honest," I say, "I hadn't really noticed whether you were stalking me or ignoring me or what. It's not really my concern."

"Then why didn't you say hi to me when you were on eight?"

"I wasn't even on eight," I say.

"Yes you were. Jake told me you were walking around the floor in circles all afternoon. In circles like some last survivor of a plane wreck in the desert or something, thinking they'll get somewhere but really just, like, the prisoner of their own physicality."

"I have no idea what you're talking about," I say, dis-missing her but intrigued with the metaphor, so I decide to parallel-path my thinking, unpacking the desert analogy and at the same time shutting down the conversation. "And I don't even know Jake."

"Clown Jake, Tom's assistant? Tom, my new boss? Jake and I knew each other in film school, that's how I got the internship."

"I may have been on eight, I'm allowed to go onto pretty much any floor I like."

"I want you to stop being mad at me and I want you to think about everything that is happening to you and ask yourself, Why am I such a dickapotamous?"

Now I try not to laugh, or smile, which is difficult because she's winking at me with her entire face.

"When people wander in the desert," she says, "with nothing to guide them, no compass or GPS or anything, they tend to just go in huge circles rather than a straight line, because inevitably one of their legs is just a little bit longer than the other."

At this I decide I've had enough of the conversation, the abject stupidity of USED POLICE CARS UNLIMITED is bothering me again, not to mention her discourse on human anatomy, and so I walk off toward Flushing. Which is when she breaks out in a half-human cackle.

I turn back and she's smiling at me and toying with the flaps of her hat.

After staying up all night drinking Herradura Gold and her getting so trashed she bangs her head on the doorjamb while trying to take pictures, and then us doing everything short of intercourse in my Hästens Vividus bed, she leaves, this time without my having to evict her and more or less in control of her bodily functions.

I call her a car and she gets dressed and I watch her and think it's ridiculous that I'm involved with a girl this young. The only sensible thing to decide is to not see her again, and that's what I do. Should I tell her this is our last conversation? I don't know if it's worth it. I stare at her feet and my hands. I need to eat.

"What are you looking at?" she asks me.

"What?" I say, pretending to be spaced out. "Your feet?"

"You're giving me a funny look."

"Am I?"

"I know you're thinking you wish you hadn't done this. You wish I hadn't shown up at that party. You wish you had more self-control than to be sleeping with someone who works with you and is younger than you and isn't even that hot."

"Yeah, no, I mean, whatever, totally," I go. "And you are hot, don't underestimate yourself, wait a second."

"Wait a second what?"

"Why would you say you're not hot? You're like Chantal Goya in *Masculin Féminin*. It's a movie by this French guy."

"I know, and Chantal Goya wasn't hot per se in my opinion. She was beautiful. She was intriguing."

About an hour ago she was naked, as was I, and she slipped one of her socks onto my dick, and she thought that was hilarious, and so she found some masking tape in a drawer, I didn't even know I had masking tape, she took two little pieces of it and she balled them up and stuck them on my sock so that it looked like it had eyes, then she grabbed her phone and was taking pictures of it. She was laughing so hard, and was so drunk, and the floor was so slick that she slipped and stumbled backward, spinning to catch herself, but it was too late. Her head hit the doorjamb, and she fell to the floor and lay there, moaning and laughing at herself. She was OK, but there was a welt near her eye, and so I cradled her for a long time, then I got some ice from the ice machine in the Sub-Zero Pro 48 and put it on the appropriate spot.

"This is crazy," she said softly. "My head is in pain but I like you."

"It is crazy," I said. Then I thought about it and said, "Wait."

"Wait, what?" she said.

"Wait, why is it crazy?"

"It just is," she said. "It just is, I can't tell you why right now, but it just is." I nodded a yes and then we went into the bedroom and went to sleep. But now it's morning and she's standing in the good-bye pose at the door, with a welt on her face, and I can hear the car service honking down below.

"That's my car," she says. I ask her if maybe we should have lunch or something, or go see a movie, or a play. She says she hates theater, it's so phony, and I think I can see tears welling up in her eyes, at least the non-swelling-up one of them.

"Maybe I shouldn't be doing this," she says softly.

"Doing what?"

"Following you. I followed you, Eric. Last night."

"You followed me? What do you mean?"

And then she tells me that she followed me from the opening to the after-party because, after all, I wasn't responding to her texts.

"Wait. How'd you know I was going to be at the opening?" I ask.

"From your e-mail," she says. I wondered for a nanosecond if maybe I had sent out a mass e-mail to the creative department touting the *Rodney* "Show Me Your Tits!" opening (my mass e-mails sometimes making it onto Agency Spy because they are so entertaining) but of course I hadn't.

"My e-mail? What e-mail?"

"You should change your password," she says, and looks away in what appears to be shame.

"What are you talking about?"

"I drink too much when I'm around you," she says. "I drink too much and I talk too much, I don't know why."

"So next time drink less and talk less."

She just says, "The car is waiting."

"Yeah, maybe, I mean, whatevs," I say.

At this point coherent communication has broken down, and I don't know what else to do so I open the door and let her out. She goes into the hallway and turns around and looks at me. She pulls something out of her Freitag messenger bag. It's a tiny little cactus.

"Here," she says. "For you."

"What is it?" I say. She gives me a look.

"It's a cactus."

"I don't like plants," I say.

"It isn't a plant. It's a *Mammillaria*," she says. "It doesn't even need water. It gets whatever moisture it desires from the air. Meaning it lives on nothing, no sustenance at all. Isn't that cool?"

When she is gone I go to the bathroom and turn the light back on (she had turned it off) and put the mini nonplant on my kitchen island. I stare at it for a long time, wondering if indeed she had meant to give it to me all along, why she hadn't earlier, why she thought it was a gift I would appreciate, what it meant, if anything, and so on. Then I call my assistant and leave a message saying I have a family emergency and won't be in. I turn off my phone and spend the rest of the day and most of the night either staring at the cactus, playing Halo, or reworking the opening sentence of my screenplay.

At some point I realize I should eat something and so I save and close the Final Draft doc and go up the street to Marlow & Sons and sit at the bar and order the Brick Chicken. I look around at everyone there. Two young women next to me are talking about whether commodities like gold and silver make good investments these days, because they are based in real things, instead of unreal things, and I push my plate away without touching the chicken or the brick, leave a hundred dollar bill on the bar, and go back across Kent Avenue to my place. Once I get there I smoke two bowls of primo sensi and take an Ambien and then a Xanax and go to sleep with my clothes on.

On the way to the office in the morning as I'm riding in
the car service over the Williamsburg Bridge I decide to call
the great dramatist and future creator of his own religion Seth
Krallman; he is after all my only friend. The views out my window and over the bridge down to the Navy Yard to the south
and Wall Street to the southwest are some of the most sweeping
in the city; for some reason I dislike them: they're trying too
hard.

I call Seth because I know that though he has been asleep
for only a couple of hours he'll take my call anyway, hoping that
I am inviting him to come up to the agency and have a look
around, prelude to my hiring him. While his phone is ringing
I try to think of something to say to him; I decide I will say I
am interested in purchasing his Range Rover. There's a certain rightness to the idea, I realize; I could drive to work every

morning, there's parking in my contract. Seth doesn't pick up, incredibly, and I leave him a message.

"Dude. It's Eric, I was just thinking, we should start a business or something. Call me."

Then in my mind I run through all the things I have going on in my life: my headhunter keeps calling me about a job in the Midwest, we're in a pitch for a new meningitis vaccine, and there's a new round of layoffs that demand some more of my and HR Lady's undivided attention.

Such as Juliette. We were supposed to fire her while I was home dealing with my "crisis." I also remember that I have to call IT and get my password changed and the whole thing with Intern sorted out; if she hacked into my e-mail that will be grounds to fire her, too. It's shaping up to be a decent day.

Juliette Chang is fifty-two. She's had some good years but she's simply an old horse that has run out of gas. I hate to say that but it's true, and that's not her fault, it's just what this business does to people. So for the past few months I've been giving her some bogus assignments at the very end of the day just to keep her busy. I will stop by her cubicle around 7:45 PM just as she is thinking of leaving (in general, no one leaves until I do; if I am not in, like yesterday, the place will be a tomb by 6:15, but if I stick around till midnight virtually everyone will stick around till midnight) and I'll say that I got a call from the Smirnoff guys and they need some new ideas for in-store point-of-sale pieces; they were thinking of a life-size cardboard cutout of a Russian girl with a thought balloon only they didn't know what the girl would be thinking in the thought balloon, could she come up with a bunch of options for a meeting tomorrow morning at 8 AM? Then she would micro-sigh, realizing that any plans she had that night were fucked, not that she had anything to do other than hang out with her cat, then an instant later she would light up with a big smile and say, "Oh sure! That sounds like a fun assignment!" I think she must have known that I was only playing with her, poking her to see if she would growl, which I was, and she never did, poor girl. At times I would think about the toxic effect I was having on her life and I would feel a form of compassion for her, and even begin to regret what I was doing. But that was not a feeling that was conducive to the financial health and wellbeing of the agency.

There's some kind of accident on Delancey and so I tell the driver to take a right on Bowery. We go north toward Houston, past the new boutique hotels and art galleries that are flocking to the area; I notice a condo tower underway and there are about two guys working there, doing nothing. I take out my phone and look at all the e-mail I didn't respond to yesterday and delete most of it. One from HR Lady says we have to meet first thing about an item of importance and she won't say what, and I assume it is about Juliette. Maybe HR went and fired her solo but I know it can't work like that, you have to have at least two company representatives in the room. Finally the traffic lightens up a bit past Fifth and from here it's a straight shot west to the Tate building.

When I get to my office she is waiting for me.

"We have something we have to talk about," HR Lady says with a mock-serious look that hides a smirky smile.

"Is she suing us for age discrimination?"

"What?"

"Juliette. Is she suing us for age discrimination?"

"Ssshh," HR Lady says, annoyed that I would even speak such words outside of our cone of silence. "No, it's not her. Something else."

We get into my office and she closes the door and looks at me.

"She's doing fine," she says.

"So you fired her?"

"No, no, she's still at the hospital."

"Wait, she tried to kill herself? What are you saying?" HR Lady has this way of talking around the truth; I've noticed it's a common advertising-based personality meme.

"Not Juliette, Sabi," she says.

Sabi? "Who's Sabi?"

"Eric," she says, giving me a look. "The production intern."

Her name is Sabi? Did I know that? "What happened to her?"

"Why don't you tell me?" she asks in a tone that I don't appreciate. I don't appreciate the barely veiled news it conveys that we are no longer on the same team. I think about it and then I say, "You know, I don't really appreciate that tone," my mind lurching in and out of clichés perhaps due to the fact I haven't eaten and I'm still as always demihard from my meds.

"Look, just tell me what happened. She's got a massive bruise on her face and she wouldn't say how she got it but she did say that she spent the night with you. Then she teared up and walked away. I realized we potentially have a situation here and so I sent her to the hospital to have it looked at."

"To have what looked at?"

"Her face."

I thought about it and decided the only thing to do was tell the truth, or as close to the truth as I could muster.

"I saw her last night," I say. "At a party. That's all there is to it."

HR Lady looks at me knowing full well that I'm witholding the sexual relations part but I'm guessing she knows better than to go there right at this moment. I am wrong.

"Did you fuck her?"

"Pardon me?"

"Did you have sex with her, Eric? I know this is uncomfortable but if you want me to get Barry involved in this I'll have to. Actually, I could get my ass in a sling for not having done so already." Barry is the company's general counsel, and the de facto president of the agency since the former president had quit, and he was one of two people in the entire building who could actually get me fired, the other being the chairman of the entire Tate Worldwide agency network. I didn't like Barry and he didn't like me. He had worked here for thirty years and was the kind of person who was loyal to the people he came up with, and he didn't like me for reasons I totally understand; I'm an asshole and not loyal to anyone, not even myself.

"No, I did not have sex with her, we just hung out a bit at my place," I say to HR.

"Are you kidding me?" she says.

I pause for a moment to watch her body twitch almost imperceptibly. "And as far as her bruise goes," I continue, "she was fucking wasted and she slipped and fell and hit her head. It had nothing to do with me."

"Really?"

"Really."

"Where were you at the time?"

"I was standing about ten or twelve feet from her."

"Doing what?" she asks. Do I tell her I was modeling her sock on my penis? Her sock she had transmogrified into something anthropomorphic?

"OK I'll tell you the truth," I say with a laugh. "We did some meth and went back to the trailer and I found out she'd been screwing my cousin Elrod and so I beat the shit out of her. Come on, this is ridiculous."

"A black eye is not ridiculous, Eric, and if a doctor says she's been, you know, *abused* . . ."

"You mean like hit? Like I hit her? You can't be serious."

"And if she says she was, you know, *raped*—and the doctor does a *test* . . ."

"A test? You mean like a DNA test? Jesus this is really getting silly."

"Of course I don't think you punched her," Helen finally says, maybe 80 percent believing it. "She fell. Or something. And I'm sure it was consensual. My God. What am I doing? I can't even think the thoughts I'm thinking right now." She sits down and looks at the floor.

"Well, she didn't have a black eye, at least when I left her this morning. She had a slight welt. Are you sure it was a black eye and not just some hip new makeupy Amy Winehousey thing?"

"I saw it," she says. "And it *is* a black eye. A bad one, too."

I stand and suddenly the blood leaves my head and goes directly into my stomach and sits there, all of it, pooling up like a superfund site. I feel like I'm going to barf so I sit back down.

"She's been hacking my e-mail," I finally say, realizing this could be my best and only defense at this point.

"What?"

"She told me this morning as she was leaving. She's admitted to stalking me. The whole thing is ugly. I think she may have caused the black eye herself. In fact, she may be insane."

"Oh great."

HR Lady looks out the window, staring at the glass curtain wall of a neighboring skyscraper, which at this time of day with the sun angling like that is just a reflection, revealing nothing. She's probably wondering why it is that guys, some guys at least, are so drawn to Crazy Girls, think about it, there's even a strip club named for them in LA, on La Brea, they go for Crazy Girls when there are good, honest, sane, all-American women sitting right in front of them. That's what I'd be thinking if I were her. My half sister, raised Episcopalian like me, is now a Muslim and living in Cairo, married to an Egyptian taxi driver, and she doesn't remember Mom being so nuts, but consider the source. My therapist, the one time I did go to a therapist, ended our one and only session by declaring that we as a family had some issues to work out in terms of our relationship to our manic-depressive matriarch, and I didn't disagree, but still I never went back, mostly because I was just telling him stories that weren't really true so how would he know. My point is that it's possible I am somehow attracted to women who are on the other side of tilt, without even knowing it, just by looking at them, one glance as it were, which is kind of how it happened that night at the bar when Intern looked at me and smiled her smile of abject joy. I felt something go wrong inside, like a glitch, or some data got hung up somewhere and never made it past the initial instruction to the OS, where I might have seen it, an error message that would have read "404: Stay Away." Instead what I get is a kind of involuntary Come Hither, a wobbly twitch in the loins, and I do go hither and with haste. What can I say? Does it really make a difference, if one chooses to be with so-called Healthy Women or so-called Total Nutjobs? We're all a little off if you ask me, it's a spectrum, which is why I initially thought HR and I were talking about Juliette Chang and the difficult time she's heading toward, thanks to me. Maybe if I spare her the karma thing, if I believed in it, that would help me out in other areas of my life; now fuck me I sound like Seth. But maybe my trouble with Intern is a sign; maybe we shouldn't fire Juliette after all? Maybe we should reconsider the whole plan?

Finally HR Lady looks back to me and says, "Well at any rate we have a situation here, we need to talk to Barry, Eric, you know that."

"You don't believe me, do you?" I moan.

"Believe you?"

"About her being crazy and hacking into my e-mail."

She pauses for about a minute and then speaks. "No, I don't really believe you. How could she do that? Is she a computer genius or something?"

"I don't know," I say. "I don't know anything about her, I didn't even know her name. All I know is she's smart as hell, I can tell you that much. She skipped two years of high school, she said, she had a perfect grade point average and even studied philosophy and cultural theory and film. She told me she made out with Slavoj Žižek. See?"

"Who?"

Now there are two things I need to say about what I just said, first being that it's not true, she never said she made out with Slavoj Žižek, she said to me that she had met him once and I understood by the look in her eye when she said it that she meant she had maybe slept with him or thought about it. And two, I know that HR Lady has absolutely no idea who Slavoj Žižek is, has probably never heard of postmodern post-Lacanian post-French Slovenian cultural theory, probably could not find Ljubljana on Google Maps.

"Who?" she says.

"This semi-Eurotrashy intellectual guy from NYU, it's not important, I'm just saying, she's a very smart girl, it's possible she's a computer hacker or knows someone who is."

I could tell that HR Lady was thinking I was a little paranoid. And, true, if you asked me to describe myself in a word or phrase I would probably say "a little paranoid."

"Maybe you're being a little paranoid," she finally says.

"I'm not! She as much as admitted it!" I say. "Why don't we get Tan to look into it?" Tan is one of our IT guys. He's autistic, or rather he has Asperger's syndrome, so he's able to hold down a job but can't really figure out the whole human interaction thing. He likes to talk to himself in the elevator, which is strange if you're the only one in it with him and you think he's talking to you. People are freaked by him and some of the younger guys had begun to call him "Cho" after that Asian dude who shot everybody up at Virginia Tech. To counter their perception and prejudice I made some posters and buttons that said TAN IS THE NEW BEIGE™ and put them around. I love the man. He's from Cambodia, his parents were killed by the Khmer Rouge. I do think he's capable of walking in here with an AK-47 and shooting the place to bits and killing us all but, first of all, so am I, and second of all, maybe that wouldn't be such a bad thing.

"Why don't we get Tan to look into it?" I say again.

"Yes, if you think so," replies HR Lady. Then she gets up and walks out. I sit there for a minute and then I go to Faco and drink three glasses of Sancerre. Then I go to Uniqlo and buy a hoodie because the temperature is dropping.

When I get back to the office I locate Tan and ask him if he could tell if someone had hacked into my e-mail. He says he most definitely was going to be there but it was raining and so he had to take the subway. I wave my hand in front of his face and then he says he could look at the log-ins. He goes onto some kind of odd-looking site, a back door into the Entourage servers that Microsoft provides for admins. He scrolls through lots of rows of numbers that I take to be the times and file sizes and so on of my e-mail. He keeps shaking his head.

"What's wrong?" I ask him.

"The way they configured this is all screwy! It's crazy!" he says in his accent. Then he dives into a diatribe about Bill (he means Gates) and Nathan (Myhrvold, the former Microsoft CTO) and how they had de-something-somethinged the preferences folder in 2002 and should never have upgraded the server-side admin features without talking to the Linux side. Then he looks deeper into the information and is reading the exact IP addresses of the people who sent me e-mail and the computers from which I checked it. It was kind of like watching your doctor stare at your X-rays while going "*hmmmm.*"

"What is it?"

"You use your phone for e-mail?" he is asking me.

"Yes."

"And you have BlackBerry?"

"Yeah but I hate it and don't use it. Mostly iPhone."

"And you have a home computer with no fixed IP and your work computer. Any other computers?

"No."

"You didn't check your e-mail from, like, a friend's computer, or a computer at a library? Or the Apple store?"

"No."

At that point HR Lady comes up to Tan's cubicle. She gives Tan a smile and says hi but I know she's one of the ones who's completely frightened of him, so she keeps her distance, as if his condition is something you can catch.

"Fuck the server side," Tan says without turning around to face her.

"You guys finding anything interesting?" she asks.

"There's another ID here pointing to the ARIN database," Tan says. He waves at a long number, then he copies and pastes it into a Google page and then he raises his left arm high in the air and, with a grand sense of theater, brings his arm down and with his index finger strikes the return key on his keyboard. He clicks on the top entry on the results page. What comes up is just a white page with a lot of info. He highlights a section of it with his mouse, touches his screen several times, says, "That's it!" and points at the screen:

NetRange: 192.168.0.0–192.168.255.255

CIDR: 192.168.0.0/16

NetName: IANA-CBLK1

NetHandle: NET-192-168-0-0-1

Parent: NET-192-0-0-0-0

NetType: IANA Special Use

NameServer: PLUTO-1.IANA.ORG

Comment: This block is reserved for special purposes.

Comment: Please see RFC 1918 for additional
    information.

Updated: 2012-4-27

"What does it mean?" I ask.

"It means that there was a log-in from a computer that isn't one of ours."

"When?"

"Yesterday."

I look over at HR Lady. See? She takes a deep breath. "So you're saying someone hacked in?"

At that Tan laughs so hard I think he is going to spit up. "No, no, of course not! Hacking! There is no such thing. Impossible. It's all Hollywood. Lulz! I set up the firewall myself. No one can get through. Impossible! Wapner in eight minutes." The last line he didn't actually say.

"Then how did they do it?"

"Oh, that's simple," he says. "They know your password."

I look at HR Lady again. See? I told you. A minute later we are in the elevator together, alone.

"Somehow she got my password?" I say to her. "How? Maybe my assistant wrote it down somewhere, she comes sniffing around my office, she sees it, who knows. I told you she was dangerous."

"Well, we don't know it was her that got into your e-mail. We don't even know if anyone did."

"But you heard him!" I am practically yelling at her. She gives me a look that is both Don't yell at me and How can you believe that crazy Cambodian? He had been found, an infant crying, bloody, and alone in the killing fields. He was rescued by an aide worker and taken to Queens, where he was raised, which to her means he can't be trusted and to me means he is a sage, although I've never been 100 percent certain of the Khmer Rouge backstory, it may only be company legend.

"I'm not sure I believe him," she says to me. "We've got some issues with him that I won't go into."

"Like what?" I ask. "You think he's going to go active-shooter-in-the-workplace on us? Tan is awesome. I love that guy."

"I can't go into it, IT is not your department."

The elevator opens and a lovely young account executive gets in. Early twenties, doe eyes, short skirt, high black boots, and a sweater that props her tits up like fresh muffins on a bamboo tray from CB2. She smiles at me. I mean of course she does, I'm someone in a position of authority, so she's acknowledging me the way any employee would, but at the same time one knows that young women are involuntarily aroused by power. Hey wassup, I smile back, with more gusto than I might have normally, if only to torture HR. The door opens at HR's floor and we get off, me with a little nod to the nameless faun. HR walks ahead of me, striding toward her office, and she flings a look back at me as if to say The way you look at women is troubling to me!

"I'm just kidding you!" I say to her, scaring her no doubt with my ability to read her mind. "I knew you were watching me, c'mon, have a laugh."

"That doesn't excuse you," she answers, and at that moment I have a sudden thought that perhaps HR Lady is bisexual or at least open to it, and not as angry as she is pretending to be; is it all just foreplay anyway for the inevitable drunken night when we have a go? No, she's far too serious, far too moral for that, this is what I like about her. She stops in the hallway in front of a big poster with the Tate logo at the bottom and on top it says FAILURE IS THE ONLY PATH TO SUCCESS™. She looks me in the eye, then looks up and down the hall to make sure we are alone.

"If I were you I'd go work from home or something before your friend gets back from the doctor. Barry and I will talk to her and we'll sort it out tomorrow. If there's an issue I'll call you."

"You're kicking me out?" I say to her.

"Yes."

"I'm, what, suspended? Double secret probation?"

"Unofficially," she says. And then, "It was Barry's idea."

"Barry's telling me to go home?"

"Yes. Barry's telling you to go home."

"Well, fuck Barry," I say. "Fuck him. Barry can't tell me to go home. Barry can't tell me shit."

"Yes he can, and he did, so go home," she says, and walks off, and I stand there looking at her not half-terrible ass.

The whole incident has bored me a bit and so I decide to go to Western Sunshine, which is a Korean massage place over by Penn Station. I've been there twice before. It would be wrong to call Western Sunshine a whorehouse because as far as I can tell you can't actually have sex with the girls, but they will give you their famed Upbeat Conclusion, which is perhaps what Western Sunshine means in Korean, and this leads me to believe that Korea is superior to all other countries on earth.

I get a cab to Eighth Avenue and as I get in I look at my device and see there is a text:

> eric eric ow my eye
> how's the cacti?
> hey dat rhymes
> where u @?

This one I don't delete because I realize I will need all the proof I can muster, in my attempt to get Intern dismissed, which I will do tomorrow, mark my word, because clearly she is unbalanced. I make a mental note to talk to Tan and see if he can't figure out a way to get a hold of her medical records, if that's possible, or even legal, I don't know, but shouldn't a company reasonably be allowed to look into the mental health and wellbeing of one of its charges? Especially one so young and new to the world of work? Ever since the TAN IS THE NEW BEIGE™ campaign Tan loves me like a brother, he'll do anything for me if I ask him. Of course there's the problem of Barry, who doesn't love me like a brother at all, and who has never liked me one bit, but that will be a minor issue: my new motto in regard to Barry being "the time is now fuck-this-shit o'clock." Once I lay out the situation for him, he will understand and get on board, because what male hasn't had the experience, at some juncture in their lurid past, of sloppy hook-upping with the all-wrong desperate needy chick who then won't stop calling you no matter how many times you tell her you aren't available, or you're gay, no you really *are* gay, you just wanted to see what all the hetero fuss was all about, and so on? Who hasn't banged the wrong girl only to have her fall on her face to get you in trouble with the law? I tell the cabbie I've changed my mind, would he mind turning around and taking me back to whence we came? Then I touch the 347 number, her number, and create a new address book entry in my phone. I label it Intern, then I change that to ??? then change it to Her then back to Intern and save it. If I get rid of her, I realize, if I succeed in that regard, however unlikely the prospect is, I will still not know the one thing I need to know: Why. Why she found me, what she wants from me, why do I have these achingy feelings for her? I resolve to find out. FAILURE IS THE ONLY PATH TO SUCCESS™, after all, it's dogma, it's doctrine, it's hanging on the wall.

part two

During my temporary exile from the Tate Worldwide head-quarters I spend the afternoon and evening at home working on my interview for *AdBeast*. *AdBeast* is the number one maga-zine for creative professionals in our industry, and they run a series in the online edition where leaders in the field (of which I am one, even though I haven't won an award in three years, and even then only on the coattails of my colleagues) are asked to interview a peer in the creative community, someone they envy or admire or, perhaps, despise. So, in order to underscore how creative and out-of-the-box my thinking really is, I decide to interview myself.

So, Eric, who starts?
I do.
Me? Why you?

I'm tired of this already.

OK, let's start. What is advertising?

Advertising is how corporations outsource their lies.

You've said that before.

Advertising is a vessel. It's nothing more than a means
to an end. For some, a paycheck that allows them
to create a family, a home, have children, grow
the human race, put more people on the planet
and live safe in the knowledge, some would say
delusion, that they are contributing to something
larger than themselves. For others, it is about
increasing the worldwide level of consumption,
and therefore wealth, of things, things we don't
need but that we believe will make us feel safe and
happy. This is a fantasy. I say a fantasy because
not only are these things we don't need, they are
also in most cases things that aren't even good
for us, are actually harming us and threatening our
survival as a species. Food, shelter, sexual relations,
and security (guns) are the only things that we
actually require in order to survive; everything
else is entertainment, or what I call Tush. The
system, in other words, has become solely about
Tush and that's why I say it is nothing but a game.
Let me give you an example. Recently one of our
clients, a manufacturer and marketer of household
products, created an extension to their famous line
of synthetic disposable diapers. They embedded

a small microchip into the diaper that can sense when the diaper is wet. The chip then immediately sends a message via Bluetooth technology to the caregiver's phone or via Twitter or whatever Mom chooses; Mom then gets a message telling her that her child's diaper needs to be changed. Now this is very interesting for a number of reasons that we discovered while doing some basic market research prior to the launch of the product. First, young mothers who we interviewed in a focus group setting all told us that this diaper innovation was hogwash, and that they were perfectly capable of knowing when their infants had wet themselves, either by touching the baby's diaper physically with their hands or by the baby's whimpering and crying, or by what some of the women called their "sixth sense" when it came to their babies, they just knew when help was needed. So right off one might think, well, this is going to be an uphill battle, these women certainly don't need this product and they don't want it either; in fact you could make the argument that they were hostile toward it because the product was somehow insulting their sense of themselves as loving, capable caregivers.

So what did you do?

Well, we looked at what the real purpose of the product was, and that was to be an object of play in the game. Remember, the basic needs have been met and so now it's all entertainment. And so the purpose of the product was not to relieve any kind of basic need but to be something one comes across in the game, a prize, and then the question is, Will she pick it up as she plays the game, as she moves to another level, or will she pass it up and pick up some other, shinier, more interesting piece of Tush? Well, obviously we want her to pick it up and put it in her shopping satchel as she moves through the game space of her life. Now in any game there are two kinds of objects: there's Treasure, and there's Bombs. Treasure are the things that get you more points in the game and Bombs are the things that allow you to transcend the barriers that are keeping you from acquiring Treasure. And here's where it gets interesting. This particular diaper is, in a way, both Treasure and Bomb. It's Treasure in the sense that it's an item whose sole use value is in being shiny, it increases world Tush, it's something a young mom can talk to her friends about at the playground or Starbucks or wherever, "Did you guys see those new diapers with the Bluetooth chip? No? Well they can actually send a text!" And the other mothers will look at her with at first disdain and immediately thereafter a sense of envy. Not envy that this mom's children are somehow more cared for than their own, no, in a sense the non-chip-diaper children are better cared for because they get some actual human attention from their mothers, they get held and touched more frequently, and so on. Instead the moms' envy will come from the fact that they will suddenly realize that they are not on the same level as this Early Adopter Mom in terms of their game status. They have fewer points, they are playing at a lower rung. And that's how it's actually a weapon, a Bomb, because the other mothers, in this version, are in fact the ones who are out there trying to beat you and get more Treasure, or keep you from getting more Treasure than they have, at least that's the way the Tush is set up in our society. And so the real purpose of the product has nothing to do with its intended usage; its real purpose is as a Treasure-Bomb by which Mother A can demean Mother B and thereby lessen the risk that Mother B will impede her success in the game. The advertising that we created for this particular product, which is now famous if not infamous, having been parodied countless times on YouTube, and called the worst advertising in history and so on, the advertising shows a group of mothers in various settings, cafés and playgrounds and a home. The mother with the chip diaper always knows first when her child has wet itself, and the other mothers are embarrassed. The tagline WHEN NATURE CALLS, WILL YOU BE THE LAST TO KNOW™? underscores this sense of embarrassment and guilt. In other words, we have created a product, if not a meme, in which we are making moms feel guilty for loving their kids: that's what Wall Street calls Creating Value.

So how did it do in the marketplace?

Sales were 800 percent higher than goal, and we've seen month-to-month lift in virtually every launch market.

All I can say is: wow.

We'll be introducing the adult version soon.

Next question: Why do you do what you do?

Hmm, OK. You mean besides the fact I make three-quarters of a million dollars a year?

Yes, besides that. How does your work feed you as a creative person?

Well, the answer is that it doesn't feed me. What's the opposite of feeding?

Starvation?

You see, what I think is interesting about what I do is that I personally don't believe in what I do, or I should say that I believe very strongly that technology (and these days advertising is completely dependent upon technology, from geo-targeting online ads to Facebook-enabled mobile apps) is actually destroying us as human

beings, it's taking away the fundamental truths
about our humanity and making us pay to get
them back: again, that's called Creating Value.

Can you give us another example?

No.

Why not?

One should suffice.

You're being a jerk now, Eric.

By taking away a mother's, one might say, natural
empathy and making her pay to get it back, we
keep the economy going. And the economy is
also just a game, a fantasy, one might even say at
this point a shared delusion. Now you might argue
that we are in charge of the game, we write the
rules, and if we don't want to destroy a mother's
ability to care for her child we can simply not sell
diapers with microchips in them. But who, I ask,
would dare to stop such a thing? Imagine if I were
to say to our clients, "Dear men of Unabrand,
does the world really need text-messaging
diapers? Shouldn't we be promoting better infant
care instead of convincing mothers that their
natural instincts are inadequate?" Well the agency
would be fired within the hour and myself along
with it. So we do nothing, in fact we cheer and
trumpet these so-called innovations, which are in
fact ruining us as human beings, and this is why
I say that the Tush, which others have dubbed

Late Capitalism, is in fact a form of madness,
a madness which will end in the slow, not even
tragic mass suicide of the human race.
And that's a good thing, I take it.
Thank you so much for the opportunity, I enjoyed our
informative discussion.
Likewise! You're really smart and interesting.
No, you are!

When finally I look up from my screen the sky is almost fully lit. Is it the morning of the day after or the afternoon of the day before? I don't know; the empty Belevedere bottle on my desk strongly indicates that I have been drinking. And my utter sense of calm in the face of yet another day on this earth without food but semi erect strongly indicates that I have taken all my pills.

Barry's office is on the fourteenth floor; HR Lady and I have agreed to meet there at 9 AM. She called me at 7:30 this morning to tell me the situation wasn't good, and I just listened patiently and then hung up, not bothering to tell her that I was going to meet privately with Barry on this, without her, because her presence in the room might skew the conversation.

When I got to work I was early and so I went directly to HR's office which is also on fourteen, the floor where all the top executives live; I liked to remind them, on the odd day when I came up here, that it was actually the thirteenth floor regardless of what they were calling it. The creative department was on three and four, account services and planning were housed on five, six, and seven; eight is for production; nine, ten, eleven, and twelve are floors that Tate formerly occupied but as they downsized over the past three years they were forced by M. Jean-Christophe, who owns the holding company that owns us, to rent out. These were now a rabbit warren of ambulance-chasing lawyers, an internet-fraud insurance company that was based in Romania, and I think a company that resold unused space on billboards.

HR Lady is in her office staring at her computer when I come in. She is twisted up and over, and her body position tells me she's in a bad mood.

"Eric," she says. "Thank you for coming in early." Then I tell her I want to meet with Barry alone, because I feel bad for dragging her into this and I want to let Barry chew me out privately and if she was around he might mince his words.

"Barry never minces anything," she says, and it is true. Barry Spinotti is an old-school adman from Brooklyn, a deranged pit bull, in other words, and everyone knows it; it's the one thing I like about him. Other things I like about him: he's fleshy, he dresses in cheap suits he buys at the Today's Man on Lexington Avenue, and he is always eating smelly food at his desk.

"Alright then I'll be honest with you," I say to her as if I am going to offer some new information, but I don't. "We all know Barry doesn't like me. Our conversation is likely to get ugly and I don't want you to have to be a party to it. He might threaten to fire me, or at least to call up Jean-Christophe and ask him to fire me, and I want to save you the embarrassment of being between us. I don't want you to have to choose between your allegiance and friendship with me and that of your boss."

She looks at me funny. Maybe she's surprised to hear me admit that we were friends, her and I, or maybe she in no way thinks of us as friends, why would she? We're not actually friends at all, even though we've gone out on occasion and drank together, but the company always paid, and maybe that's a good definition of what friendship is: having a drink with someone when it's on your own dime and not your firm's. By that count we were not friends at all. And complicating things was the time we got thoroughly trashed and made out for five seconds by the entrance to the F train, although that never happened, and because I imagined it I sometimes think it did. What would transpire, I wonder, if in fact I said to her: stop, Helen, please let's stop this cruelty, this soul-crushing work of ours, forget about your boyfriend who nobody has ever seen, forget about this stupid business and this stupid town, let's move to Sebastopol and get dumb jobs and just live like people do. What would she say? Probably nothing, probably she would think I was nuts, after all she already thinks I am nuts, but maybe she wouldn't think that, maybe she doesn't think that, maybe she thinks we are in the same boat, sinking together.

"It's bad," she finally says.

"What is?"

"She never came back to work from the hospital, she was treated and went home. I spoke to her last night, she said she was tired and needed to rest but would be back in today."

"That doesn't sound so bad," I say.

"Let me finish," she says. "I don't want to join you in Barry's office any more than you want to go there. I spoke to a doctor at Mount Sinai and he said her contusion isn't serious, that it will heal normally, but that it was possibly caused by the impact of a fistlike object."

"What's a fistlike object?" I ask. There's something vaguely porno about the term, and normally I would have brought this up in a slightly offensive way but I decide that now is not the time; indeed I take that as a sign of positive growth. She looks at me as if I am an idiot. "No, seriously, I'm totally lost, please help me," I beg.

"She was punched in the face!" she says.

"Really?"

"There's no point at this point in lying to me, Eric!" she spits, and I realize that it's all on the line now so I decide to go emo on her. I pause and look her directly in the eye, or eyes, as it were, my eyes to her eyes, rights to lefts and vice versa.

"I'm only going to ask one thing of you," I say. "Well, actually, two things."

"What are they?"

"No, one thing, just one, I take that back. Because I can't ask you to simply believe me, can I, since after all as you know I'm a liar. You've heard me lie countless times to all those people we've had to fire this year, not to mention our clients, so why would you believe anything I said to you now?"

"What is it?" she says.

"All I ask of you is: let me see Barry by myself for fifteen minutes. I promise, this whole thing will work itself out."

"You're repeating yourself," she says, not blinking even once.

Heading down the hall toward Barry's corner I can begin to smell the smoke. Despite decades of legislation in this area, Barry still smokes cigarettes in his office. When I get there he is on his speakerphone, eating a greasy egg-and-sausage sand-wich, sucking on a Newport Light and leaning over toward his Smoke Eaters air filtration device, which sits on the edge of his big black lacquer desk which must have been quite fashionable designwise in, like, 1983. The Smoke Eater (possible tagline: LET THEM EAT SMOKE™, no, not that, maybe ENABLING YOUR ADDICTION ACCOMPANIED BY AN ANNOYING HUMMING SOUND™) looks like a rice cooker, but a little smaller, like one of those white noise machines you put next to your bed so that you can't hear the screaming down the hall, and it whirrs to a start when Barry presses the top of it and blows smoke toward its round gob, which sucks it in with an unhealthy whine. What a dis-gusting man, I think, how many awful chemicals there must be lodged in every crevice of every tissue of his body, which may be why at sixty-whatever he's still working here, still alive, pre-served in chemicals, he'll never die because technically he's al-ready dead, he's undead, he's pickled by fear, lies, and nicotine.

"I gotta get off the goddam phone," he says to whoever he's talking to. "Nye," he says to no one in particular but since that is my name I know he must mean me, "get your hipster ass in here." Then he stuffs his breakfast sandwich into the fleshy maw located in the center of his colorless face and keeps pushing until most of it is jammed in there and then he begins chewing, bent down over the desk so that the egg yolk drips out and runs down his chin like yellow chicken cum onto the crumpled tin foil in front of him. "Where's your cohort?"

"I wanted to talk to you first, just the two of us," I explain.

"Fine, good, now I can chew your ass out in private."

"That's what I figured, sir."

"Close the door and don't call me sir. I know you hate my guts." Barry is worth at least fifty or sixty million since the agency was sold to La Groupe S. A., the holding company that owns the holding company owned by M. J-C.

"I don't hate your guts, Bar," I say, "I love you," and at the moment, watching him shovel himself, this is basically true. He puts down the last bit of his egg-and-sausage, sucks at the ends of his fingers, and reaches for the smoldering Newport sitting in the battery-powered vacuum-action ashtray that sits next to the Smoke Eater. He takes a long drag on the butt and leans over toward the machine and exhales into it again like it's some girl or cat he's trying to get high; I almost expect him to tongue the thing.

"I assume you don't mind if I smoke," he says, probably reading from a script he wrote for legal reasons; by sitting here I've clearly given up my right to take action. "They won't even let me smoke outside the building anymore, can you believe that? Somebody complained about the secondhand out on the sidewalk. It's New York Fucking City, it's Tenth Fucking Avenue."

"Times change, I guess."

"Oh shut the fuck up you asshole," he says to me, and I know that this is going to go extremely positively, because we'll end up laughing about the whole thing, the two of us, he'll agree that the girl deserved it, even if I didn't hit her, and he'll tell his dumb twat secretary with the bazooms out to here to make us a reservation at Keens for lunch. I can almost taste the Kobe beef burgers and a glass or four of good Chianti to wash it down.

"Listen, you can thank me later, alright, but for the time being you're gonna have to lay low."

"Thank you for what, Barry?" I ask. "Other than your general awesomeness."

"Wipe that smile off your face, you prick," he says, meaning it, having fully cleaned up his face and hands and finished the Newport off with a last desperate draw before squishing it into the bowl. "You think this is some kind of a joke? I got Helen coming in here with this. I had to basically scream and yell at her all morning."

"Helen?" I asked. "Helen and I are friends."

"It's not personal," he goes on. "But she thinks that nineteen-year-old you punched is gonna bring an action or something if we don't treat her right, which I am not prepared to do."

"Punched? Is that what you think, too?"

"Stop laughing at me, this is serious."

"I'm not laughing at you, a and b) she isn't nineteen, she's older than that although I don't know how much older, and c), I didn't punch anyone," I say. "I've never punched anyone in my life."

"So you want to explain what happened?"

"She slipped and banged her head on a door in my apartment, she was really drunk."

"Well the fucking doctor she saw says otherwise."

"I don't know what to tell you, Barry. I had relations with her, yes, I admit that, but that was before we hired her. And it's not going to happen again, believe me. But I never hit her."

"Except with your dick."

"Well, yes, true, I did hit her with my dick, so to speak." Jesus, why didn't I think of making a reality show about this guy?

"Then you're dumber than even I thought."

"Honestly, Barry, I figured you'd understand and help me out here."

"Me?" he says. "Why would I help you out?"

"Because . . . we're both trying to save this place from going under," I say. "We're in this thing together."

"No we aren't," he answers quickly and with a bitter smirk. "I'm just working until my contract runs out, at which time I get another quarter-million shares, and then I'm gone. I got four houses, I could give a shit if this place burns to the ground. And you're just fucking around until your next job offer, or until your father croaks and leaves you his Berkshire Hathaway stock so you can sell it and stop working and start making independently wealthy films or whatever it is you plan on doing. So cut this nonsense about saving the agency, you don't give a rat's ass about the agency and neither do I. Neither does anybody and that's why we're in the muck we're in."

He sighs for about a minute and a half and then looks out his window to the street below, to the press of humanity ebbing their way toward a morning of sadness and cubicles, with occasional relief provided by the internet.

"Was she a good fuck at least?" he finally says.

"We were drunk, Barry, we didn't even screw. And I didn't know she would hack my e-mail, that she would worm her way in here, I don't know exactly how she did that, either, she may have blown Tom in his office, he won't tell me."

"She blew who in his office?"

"I don't know if she blew anybody in anybody's office, I'm just saying I think she may be a little nutty."

"Well you gotta understand something," he says, jabbing at the smoke-filled air in front of my face. "When I was your age, we could get away with this kind of shit, and you can't get away with it anymore. Plain and simple. There's only one thing we can do."

"What's that? Get rid of her?"

"No. You. We have to get rid of you." He lets it sit there for a long beat, longer than he needs to.

"OK," I say, "I guess it is what it is."

"No, you're reading me wrong," he says, motioning with his flabby arm for me to sit back down. "I can't fire you, you're too valuable, you're too good at your job. Look, we searched high and low to find a sucker who was dumb enough to run this shitshow, a trendy cluck like you who looked good in press photos and would do what none of us around here had the stones to do, what M. J-C made a requirement of his bestowing of our stock options upon us. I couldn't do it, nobody here could do it. We needed somebody of your cloth, somebody who gets into that upbeat TED bullshit and believes they're saving the fucking planet and so on."

"Yeah," I said quietly, his words swimming around in the space inside my head.

"So how many left you gotta can? Two?"

"A few," I say. "A couple few more, I'd rather not talk about it."

"I need you to get out of here, go away for a week. Let this whole thing cool off. There's a big shoot in LA, and the client's not happy."

"Yeah, new FreshIt Air Freshener product launch, but I was not planning on going, there's too much that requires my attention right here."

"No there isn't, you barely come to work. Here's the plan: you go out to the shoot, schmooze the idiots, keep the account, by the time you're back this whole thing has gone away."

"Done," I said.

"You stay at Shutters? I love that place, very classy."

"Well at least we're aligned on that," I say. And then he slides open his desk drawer and roots around inside it and I take this as my cue to get up. As I'm turning to go he hands me a business card.

"Wait a second, fuckface. I don't know if he's still in business but you gotta go see Dr. Look before you go to the coast."

"Dr. Look?"

"He's a shrink but he's not a bad guy. You gotta go see him for insurance and legal purposes, get a clean bill on your mental health, it won't take ten seconds."

"Barry," I say, "I didn't hit her. I swear I didn't."

"Maybe you didn't," he says. "Or maybe you did and you just don't remember because you don't want to admit it to yourself. You've repressed it like in those movies."

"That's ridiculous," I say.

"When I was eight years old I was fucked in the ass by my uncle Charlie, and I didn't remember a thing about it until last year."

Suddenly he bursts out laughing. "I'm kidding you. Dr. Look will fix this, alright? Now thank me for saving your job and get the fuck out of my office."

"I'll call you from LA," I say as I leave. "And thank you."

"No, you won't call me," he says as he lights another Newport. "And if you do I won't pick up."

As I'm stepping onto the elevator to return to my office, HR Lady comes rushing after me. I pretend to hit the "open" button but it doesn't matter as she manages to wave an arm between the doors and they part. I tell her I'm on my way home post-Barry and then to LA.

"Now?" she says.

"Yes," I say. "I'm going home to pack."

"Aren't you forgetting something?" she asks.

"Am I? What?"

"Juliette."

The elevator opens on three and HR holds the door for me so that I'll follow her out toward our grim task. But I don't.

"Eric, this is your floor," she says.

"I know," I say. "Why don't you take this one yourself?"

She cocks her head to the side, says "You know I can't do that. You're her boss, you have to do it, I have to accompany you, those are the rules."

"Well maybe we could put it off till I get back from LA?" I say. The elevator starts beeping that annoying beep because she's still holding it open.

"What good would that do?" HR says. "At this point Juliette probably knows what's going on, waiting will only make it worse."

"I get that, OK, so what about just not doing it."

"Not doing what?"

"Not firing her."

HR looks at me, the doors start to push in slowly against her arm, and the beeping gets louder. "We have to," she says.

"According to who?"

"Are you really asking me this?" she says.

Our eyes lock for a moment, a moment of truth as it were, and maybe she's picturing it, the same thing I am, the refusal to fire Juliette being the first volley, ending with me gathering the troops in the fishbowl and announcing that the cruel game is over, the departed will be returning soon, and then HR and I standing there, raising our arms in heroic triumph as a light applause ripples through the group, turning into a thunderous roar of gratitude.

"Eric, this thing is going to take my arm off if you don't get out here," she says.

When we get to my office, Juliette Chang is waiting dutifully in a piece of uncomfortable midcentury furniture. She has her laptop propped up on her knees and she's working or at least trying to appear like she's working when we arrive. My assistant gives me a look, I know that look, it's the "You're really late for a meeting" look, and indeed Juliette's been waiting since nine to chat with me, she thinks about Smirnoff or something. But a forty-five-minute wait is the least of her worries, and it's nothing compared to what I've already put her through; in fact, it's so respectful for me to even show up it's almost like I'm promoting her, giving her a gift, a bottle of pinot or a few days off or something.

She sees us approaching and looks at me with a big smile; it's the broadest and phoniest of smiles and she's been leaning on that smile since she landed at Tate right out of college thirty years ago. Then I see her eyes flit over to HR, she sees the two of us walking together, our strides in synch at this point, and now she knows. She has to know; she's known all along, she's known since the day I got here and started firing all the people her age, but the smile stays pasted on, exactly the same, only the degree of effort changes.

A minute later we're sitting in my office, Juliette and HR and me, and the door is closed. We all get seated and she is just staring at me.

"I'm, um," I say, not really looking at her. "We're in a tight position and we, um, due to some client requests we, um, we have to make some deep cuts. I'm very sorry to say this but we're going to have to—"

"If you think I didn't see this coming you're wrong," Juliette spits out. "For weeks now, months even, I knew. Everyone knows."

"I'm really sorry, Juliette," I say. HR begins her speech about our very generous severance package we're currently offering but Juliette won't let her even get to the benefits part.

"I've come to this building almost every single day of my life for thirty years," she starts. "I have a sister upstate who suffers from severe diabetes and she can't work and so I support her and her child."

"Juliette," I say, not having any idea why I am interrupting her or what I might say next.

"You know at my age I'll never get another job in this business. You know how much this means to me and yet you went to all these pains to make it look like you were my friend and we were on the same team."

"I didn't want you to . . . I wanted you to have a . . ."

"Have a what?" she asks. "A sense of reality? Dignity?"

"Juliette," HR says softly, wiping moisture from her eyes with the base of her palm. "Let's just try to—"

"Try to what?" Juliette implores. HR hands her a folder of legal stuff to look over but Juliette doesn't take it. Both her hands are gripping her laptop tightly and I think she has accepted it and is about to stand up, so I lean forward putting more weight on my toes in anticipation of standing up at the same time as her, and I am wondering if I should shake her hand and thank her for all she's done for the agency or if perhaps I should hug her since she had divulged so much personal information to me just now. I really don't know what to do or say and suddenly I have the thought that I wish there were a remote with which I could put Juliette on pause and ask HR Lady what the most appropriate response should be from me at this time, insincere intimacy or the wise, knowing strength of a real leader, a firm handshake and I look her in the eye and say, human being to human being, "I'm an asshole and deserve to die, I know this now" or something to that effect. What is, after all, the proper way to bring about real change? The proper way to behave in the face of a human face? But before I can formulate what my action will be in response to all this, she begins to speak again.

"Eric," she says, "I have one thing to ask of you."

"What is it?" I say.

"Please don't fire me."

This is not at all what I expected.

"Without this job I really don't have anything," she goes on. "I don't know what to tell my sister or her son."

"I'm so sorry," I say.

"If you were, you wouldn't be doing this."

I look over at HR. Is it too late to take it all back? I give her a what-can-we-do-now look but she won't make eye contact with me. I look back at Juliette.

"There's nothing I can do," I say. "It's just how it is."

"I've got an idea," Juliette says, almost happy about it, she always had lots of ideas. "I make a lot of money, I'll take a pay cut. I'll take a 50 percent cut. Isn't that what you have to do, reduce the staff by half? At least that's the rumor going around. I'll take a 60 percent cut. Please. Will you think about it?"

Then HR looks at me and there's a silence and it's clear I'm supposed to say something, but I don't know what to say. What

I want to say is "OK, I accept your offer of a 50 percent pay cut, it's reasonable and well considered, after all, you make more than twice what anyone else at your level makes so I don't see why we can't—" But HR would cut me off and remind me that I don't have the authority to accept her offer, or to make her a counter offer, I don't really have any authority at all.

At this point Juliette is looking at me the way you would look at someone next to you after a car accident and things are going in very slow motion but you realize that you and the other person are alive although you don't know yet if you are injured.

"Juliette, I'm sorry, but Eric doesn't have the authority to accept such an offer at this time," HR is saying.

"Why not?" Juliette asks. "He's the Chief Idea Officer."

"Yes, but anything like that would have to go through corporate and be approved by corporate!"

"Well OK then, I'll go back to work and you'll let me know when it's approved," Juliette says.

"Who's corporate?" I ask HR. "Aren't we corporate?"

Then I'm giving her that what-the-fuck-are-we-doing head shakey look but she's already on her BlackBerry calling somebody, I'm guessing corporate, and Juliette and I sit there looking at her and waiting but nobody is answering on the other end.

When she turns back toward us there are tears in her eyes.

"I'm talking about the holding company!" she says, "In France! They're the ones making these decisions. Please. It's not up to us! They look at salary versus client billing hours vis-à-vis the AOR contracts and they make the determinations and create their kill list. Juliette, you have to understand this is not about us!"

"How could it not be about you?" she says. "You're the ones doing it."

"Because we have to!" HR says.

"You have to?"

"We have to because if we don't, we'll get fired," she says. "You have to understand."

"And also, full disclosure, we wouldn't get our bonuses," I say, and at this HR's jaw drops and she stares at me.

"That's a breach, Eric," she says. "You've got to leave now. This is done, it was decided months ago. Please, please understand, Juliette. There's nothing anyone can do." And then she turns back to me. "Please go."

But I just sit there, unable to move.

At my inaction Juliette looks at me and I try to impart, by the letting go of my facial muscles, the sense of abject melancholy that has taken over my entire being. I realize, of course, that what HR is saying is entirely true, that were I to even attempt to make some kind of promise to Juliette right now, and send her back to her cubicle with a sense of hope, it would be completely disingenuous, not to mention self-serving, as it would only delay the inevitable, because anything I would say corporate would overrule, and she would only have to go through the humiliation all over again. I am trying to impart all of this with a single look of resignation, and Juliette to her credit gets it, she realizes it's really happening now, and she begins to weep, to herself at first, the sobs pushing up from somewhere very deep within her, someplace she probably didn't even know existed, a heretofore unknown sub-basement of her psyche. These fears had lived down there for so long that when they finally rise to the surface they are large and scary and uncontrollable, and she is sucking in air so hard and fast it looks like she is drowning. I want to say something comforting now, but it seems too late, it will only be hypocritical, so I look away, out the window. HR puts her BlackBerry away, leans in toward Juliette, and reaches her hand out toward the woman and it finally comes to rest on her knee, which is covered in a black stocking. Finally we look at each other and HR gives me a kind of "What should I do now?" shrug with her shoulders and eyes. I mimic her gesture back to her like a mirror and we sit there sharing the discomfort, or rather HR's discomfort because at this point, to be perfectly honest, I am too numbed by my present numbness to feel discomfort; this is just something that is happening, to all of us. Then HR gets up and goes out and waves to Damon and Terry and now I am alone with Juliette for a moment. She has let go of her laptop and it has fallen to the floor and she is grabbing the arms of her chair, trying to hold on. I have no idea how long I am sitting there, trying to think of anything other than what is going on, thinking about all the things I have to do today, including making sure there is a Prius available to rent in LA and a beach-facing nonsmoking room at Shutters, when the two stolid African-Americans are in the office and they are taking hold of Juliette and peeling her panic-hewn fists from the arms of the chair. They walk her slowly and wobblingly out of my office and over to the elevators. Meanwhile my assistant has retrieved Juliette's jacket from her cubicle and is handing it to her as they pass, and is hugging her—she is still sobbing—and then they turn the corner and I can't see them anymore.

Dr. Look's office is in a downtrodden two-block stretch of Lexington just north of Citicorpse. Every other block in this part of midtown has been razed for the erection of skyscraping hubris-temples to ill-begotten wealth but something went horribly wrong here and the block was never properly developed. I get to the address on the card that Barry shoved at me and see that Dr. Look's office, also known as Midtown Health, Inc, sits two floors above an Egyptian souvenir and cheap-luggage shop that must be a front for something, possibly black-market kidneys, or passports. I had heard, in the couple of years that I have been at Tate, certain folkloric tales about the company's founder, Windham Tate, being quite a philanderer, if that is the word, back in his day, which would have been the '60s and '70s; how he fucked every young secretary in the place and how there was actually a line item to pay them off if they went after him in court or such, and how he even had a phony doctor who would claim they were all unbalanced. It was making sense now; Barry had sent me to his fixer. I go up the stairs and try the door and it's locked and so I figure that indeed Dr. Look has moved if he had ever been here at all, if he had ever existed; it could easily be some kind of joke only Barry would find funny. Then I see there's a buzzer hanging loose from its wire, and taped to the buzzer is a business card, the same one I have in my hand, only this one is stained and dog-eared. I ring the buzzer, or rather I press it, I have no way of knowing if it is ringing or not. I assume it isn't. But then as I am about to leave, the door opens. A young goateed man in his midtwenties stands there and stares at me funny, shaking his head as if there's something wrong.

"Sorry, I was expecting the delivery guy, you're not the delivery guy, are you?"

"No," I say, "I'm not the delivery guy."

"Three days now I'm supposed to get some papers from a conference I recently attended, I'm beginning to think they just tossed them in the river."

"I'm, I guess you would say, looking for Dr. Look," I offer.

"I'm Dr. Look, is there anything I can help you with?"

"I was referred by my company. Tate? They said I should see a Dr. Look and I guess that's you."

"Oh, of course, come in," Dr. Look says. He extends his hand and I'm thinking he doesn't seem old enough to have gone to college and medical school unless he was some kind of a prodigy, which maybe he is. We go inside the space, which is actually a railroad apartment that was never renovated, never turned into a drivers ed school or a CPA's office like the rest of them on this block. "Take a seat," he says, gesturing to an old black couch that has been repaired with duct tape. I don't know what else to do so I sit on the edge of it and watch while he opens and closes the drawers on a row of filing cabinets that take up one wall. On the other wall there's nothing but a clock, one of those plastic cat clocks where the eyes move back and forth and the tail wags every second. Eventually he finds whatever he's looking for, a sheet of paper, and turns toward me. "Here it is."

"Here what is?"

"The form." He takes it and sits down at an old desk and hunts for a working pen. He finds one and scribbles on the sheet of paper, then signs his name at the bottom and stands.

"Done."

"What's done?"

"The paperwork."

He comes around the desk and hands the form to me and I take it and look at it.

"What is it?" I ask.

"You came to me, we spoke at length, I conducted an extensive psychological examination, and then I deemed you fit," he says. I had heard there were scam doctors like these in New York, the ones actors went to when they needed to pass a drug test before working on a movie. I look at the paperwork.

"You mean mentally fit? How do you know I'm mentally fit if we didn't even speak?"

"We don't have to talk about it unless you want to talk about it," he says.

"Talk about what?"

"Whatever it is you did."

"But I didn't do anything."

"It's a formality," he continues. "Let's assume you kicked a door in, or in a pique of anger you threw a chair out a window. Or tossed your computer at a wall. Screamed at a colleague, threatened to kill someone, took a shit in your boss's office, or any of a million other things you might do and that people in stressful jobs do everyday, and let's say some overly sensitive person reported it internally to the human resources department, and for insurance purposes your company needs to vet you as not insane, so you come to see me. The liability requires it."

"But I didn't lose my temper," I say. "I never lose my temper."

"No?"

"No. I don't even have a temper to lose."

"Well then perhaps this is merely meant to be prophylactic."

"In what way?"

"Perhaps someone is worried you might possibly lose your temper at some point in the future."

"But couldn't anyone possibly lose their temper?" I say. Dr. Look pauses for a moment to consider this, nodding with a mock seriousness he didn't even know was mock.

"I suppose. But that's really none of my concern." He then reaches out his hand to shake mine, indicating that the office visit is over. I stand dutifully and take his hand and shake it for the second time. Then I look at the form again.

"It says here we met three times for one hour each time."

"That's right, that's what the insurance company requires."

"But I've only been here for five minutes. And you're going to bill my company for three hours at, what, what's your hourly?" I ask him, knowing it's rude but going there anyway.

"Four-fifty," he says.

"So you're going to charge my company thirteen hundred and fifty dollars to deem me mentally fit without even talking to me?" I say, repeating the obvious, and with a tinge of disbelief.

"Would you rather you had to come here three separate times?" he asks. "Who has the bandwidth to do that these days?" I don't say anything, I stand there looking at him. Then I look at the form again. Through the jargon I spy a number from the *Diagnostic and Statistical Manual of Mental Disorders*, known as the *DSM*, that psychiatrists use: 310.83. I've studied the *DSM* before and I know what the classification means.

"Isn't 310.83 Borderline Personality Disorder?" I ask. "I thought you said I was fit as a fiddle?"

He looks at me with more mock mock-concern than before and then slowly crosses over to an easy chair that looks like it had been sitting out in the rain for a year.

"Sit down," he says quietly. "Why don't we begin?"

I sit back down on the couch, which I now realize is a divan like you would see in an actual psychiatrist's office, with a headrest at one end. It's then that I look around for a diploma on the wall. I find one and squint at it.

"Harvard," he offers. "Psychiatry MD with a PhD in behavioral studies."

"Really," I say. "That's great."

"This isn't my main office," he says as I look around. "My main office is downtown."

"I see."

"So why don't you tell me what happened?" he says, and there's something about his tone, something strong and reassuring yet at the same time anxious, as if he is hiding some kind of horrible career-destroying event in his past, something that got him here, a character-defining backstory that doesn't get revealed till the end of Act Two, and this comforts me; I want to know more.

"Well . . ."

Then a long silence hangs between us and I realize for the first time that noises from the street can be heard, cars whooshing by and horns and a siren in the distance. An argument, in Spanish, or is it Cantonese, becomes barely audible, too, filtering up from below. Dr. Look reaches down to his feet where one of those white noise machines sits half-hidden under the skirt of the easy chair. It's a round gray cylinder about the size of a small pound cake with a single switch on the side of it. He feels around for the switch and then flicks it, keeping his eyes on me the whole time, and the machine begins making its patented, airy, noise-canceling, oatmeal-colored sound, and then all the sounds of the street fade away into oblivion.

I sit there listening to the machine (possible tagline: SILENCE = JUST TOO FUCKING FRIGHTENING FOR THE TIMES WE LIVE IN^{TM}) fighting the effort of my mind to cancel that sound out, too, and so there we are bathed in a kind of delusional quietude, a silence built of a protracted death rattle, and I don't think I've ever felt such peace.

"I lied earlier," I say. He waits. "They think I hit someone," I continue, "which I didn't, I'm sure of that, although I was heavily intoxicated at the time, so perhaps it's possible that I pushed her, although I don't think I did, in fact I know I didn't. But it's all quite a mess."

My gaze remains fixed on him to note his reaction, to see how far I can push this fallen man into moral lassitude and fraud.

"Hmmm," he says.

"I mean it's interesting, because they're saying I punched someone in the face, and she's saying I punched her in the face apparently, and even though that's false there's a certain amount of truth to it. Not her, but other people."

"Who?" he says quietly, with a tilt of his head to suggest I lie down on his Viennese divan. I take the cue and lean back, putting my head flat on the couch, and now I'm staring up at an old partially rusted tin ceiling, sections of it missing and replaced by plywood painted the same creamy beige.

"A woman I work with," I go. "A girl, really."

"You hit her."

"OK, for the sake of argument let's assume I did," I say. He doesn't give me the pleasure of a reaction, and so I can't tell if he thinks it is a grave and terrible thing I've done or if this is the smallest and least worrisome act of random violence that he's ever come across. Of course it's also possible that he knows I'm fabricating, since I've never hit anyone, certainly not a woman and most definitely not the intern, but since I do happen to know that I am an extremely effective liar, and no one ever knows when I'm lying, ever, with the possible exception of the time said intern called me on my not getting her text message.

"Go on," he says.

"She's nineteen or twenty or something, maybe older, I don't know, she's an intern at the firm," I tell him, laying out the basic facts of the story as simply as I can. "I've slept with her, sort of, and I enjoyed it and all, but the thing is, the thing that I can't understand, is why it is I seem to have fallen in love with her." He doesn't say anything now and so I feel compelled to go on. "I don't even know why I fooled around with her, apart from the fact that I was horny, and she's funny, but I'm always horny and there are lots of funny girls and I masturbate eight or sometimes ten times a day in an attempt, one might call it vain, to rid myself of my erection, or at least partial erection, that I have had for quite some time now, nearly a year, ever since I started taking the medications I am taking in the current combination I am taking them." I stop here, figuring this is enough shrink candy for one visit.

"You celebrated yourself in various ways," he says. "It's normal."

"I've masturbated in my office at work, I've masturbated in an empty lot in the middle of the night, I've masturbated in the back of taxi cabs, in stairwells of department stores, in airport bathrooms, I've masturbated on airplanes, I've masturbated while driving on the New York State Thruway and looking at lewd photos on my iPhone." I'm really laying it on thick.

"Why do you think that is?" he inquires, testing me, but I don't take the bait.

"I guess you would say that I have a strong sex drive. Of course I can get sex pretty much whenever I want it, and I have paid for it on occasion, I work all the time so I don't always have the bandwidth, as you call it, for dating. When I do date normally I date actresses and models. I meet them often in my job, and I make a good deal of money, so they're attracted to me. I've never really had a relationship with anyone and I'm thirty-three. I guess that's not so weird since the advent of video games and reality television, not to mention that new porno app everybody is talking about, thirty-three is the new nine."

Then I put an unexpected twist into the story, a Henry.

"I guess it all goes back to my mom," I say and then, without thinking what's coming next, there it is, sliding out of my mouth. "She died in a car accident when I was ten years old. I saw the whole thing."

The rest of it just writes itself. "I was standing in our front yard and my mom was driving down the street. In my mental re-creation of that day I surmise that she was drunk because when she got to our house instead of slowing down to let a garbage truck pass she must have hit the gas instead of the brake. She lurched forward right into the front of the truck as it was zooming by."

I figure this would be an excellent place for a pause and so I put one there. I look at him and wait, wondering why I am making up all these tales when there are perfectly valid truths I could be telling him; my father's emotional rectitude (my sister's phrase) or my mother's actual illness. Dr. Look doesn't say anything for a while. Then: "It must be very difficult for you to speak of these things," he says quietly.

Nothing has changed in the room but for some reason now it seems dark, as if many hours have passed in the last minute and a half. He shifts in his chair and suddenly I'm worried that he is going to come over and try to touch me, perhaps put a hand on my shoulder, but he doesn't.

"So then what happened?"

"With the intern? You mean after I punched her? I got her a towel and some ice. I'm totally lying," I say. "I didn't punch anyone."

"I know that," he says, "but we're talking about your mother now. So she was killed in an accident."

"I ran up to the car and pulled the door open and screamed loud enough to wake my dad, who was inside the house, asleep in the dark in front of the TV"—I'm not a narrative innovator in any way—"and then I grabbed her bloody hand and pulled her from the wreck, only it was too late. She died in my arms right there on our street, which was called Magic Elm Drive."

"Your mother died in your arms?" He repeats my statement in the form of a question. "On the street in front of your house?"

I nod yes. We remain silent for a long time. Long enough for me to realize that the died-in-my-arms line was a bit too much. "Was she heavy?" he finally asks. "Your mom? What was her name?"

"She was a bit chubby, yes, as I was growing up," I say. "The body is only a vessel, an avatar of our actual selves."

"What I'm wondering about," he now says, "is how at age ten you managed to pull a somewhat, as you say, chubby woman from a wrecked car, and hold her in your arms while she died."

"I was a pretty strong kid," I say. "I lifted weights. I worked out."

"Alright," he says, leaning forward. "I find it of interest that you would tell me this story."

"You're a shrink, yes? Isn't this what people do?"

"I mean such a blatantly untrue story."

"I was testing you," I say.

"And the girl that you punched," he goes on, "you said that she is quite attractive, is that right?"

"Why do you ask?"

"Why do you ask why I ask?"

"I don't see what her relative attractiveness has to do with it. Because my mom was not attractive? I'm confused."

"About?"

"Everything."

There's a long silence. Then he says, "Perhaps you blame yourself for your mother's death, even though you had nothing to do with it. You blame yourself for hitting your girlfriend even though you did not hit her. And you blame yourself for hurting people at your firm even though that too is a situation you cannot control."

"How did you know about that?" I asked him, even though I knew the answer.

"I think we're going to have to stop for today," he says.

"But I thought I got an hour," I reply. This guy really had his scam going. Not that we both don't.

"And it appears we've gone over," he says, pointing at the clock on the wall, and from my prone position I crane around but can't really read the clock since it doesn't have any numbers and from where I am a three could easily be a six or a nine is a twelve. So I sit up and try to focus on the clock with its inane swinging cat eyes, and he's right, somehow we have gone over, way over, although it's also highly possible that while I wasn't looking he got up and moved the little hands. As I stand he passes me his business card and I take it, look at it, he has scrawled on it the time of our next appointment: tomorrow at two.

As I'm walking back to the office I realize I left the mental fitness form on his desk; this was either an oversight on my part or, now that we had begun actual therapy, perhaps he didn't mean for me to take it. I turn onto Fifty-third and pass a falafel cart and so I stop and get a chicken shawarma. I stand there watching this protoslave slopping ash-white lettuce and toma-toes onto a slab of blanched pita, then he dumps some pieces of genetically modified chicken flesh on top of that, and then he smothers the whole thing in a thick white fatty sauce. My plan is to take it to my office and eat it there, but instead I stop about a block farther down the street and just stand there stuffing it into my mouth and chewing; I realize this is the first meal I've had in almost a week, I need to eat more slowly. I get about half of it down and then I stuff the remainder into my mouth and watch as goo drips down onto the curb. Then I wipe my chin with my sleeve and head back to work; within a few steps I don't feel well. At the corner of Forty-ninth and Broadway I stop and involuntarily upchuck onto the sidewalk; what was I thinking eating this shit? I finish expectorating my Jihad Chicken and get up and stand there looking around as if vomiting on the street is something I want some fucking attention for, people, hello, look at me. Then the light changes and I cross the street toward the office; to complete the picture I take out my phone and make a call to a friend as if nothing at all could ever be out of the ordinary. I redial the last number in my phone, which it turns out is the Magic Man, Seth Krallman, his own line of digital yoga mats coming soon, and as I'm walking south I tell him via the phone the one thing I've been meaning to tell him for days now, but didn't have the chance to, and that is that I really should buy his car.

After hanging up I wander into the Starbucks on Thirtieth about a block from my office and sit down and wait for Seth to swing by in his Range Rover, which he has agreed to sell me for a yet-to-be-determined price. I came in here because I thought I was going to throw up again, and ended up sitting in the bathroom for a good forty-five minutes just waiting. Then I felt guilty using their bathroom for so long, and so I bought a green tea and sat down and called Seth and told him I wouldn't be coming to Brooklyn, that he should bring the car to me.

"What am I, homes, like your freakin' delivery bitch?" he says at me with a laugh but I can tell he isn't happy about it.

"I'll add a c-note to the price for your trouble," I tell him and he says OK.

An hour later he pulls up and honks outside. I clean up my spot at the table, throw the remains of my tea away in the hole in the counter where the half-and-half is, and go outside. I am the one who replaces the will to survive with the need to consume, I tell Seth. He asks me if I am OK and then we drive downtown.

"Without me there would be nothing but the pure anguish of being alive, which is too difficult to bear, so I am providing a pubic service." I use the word "pubic" as a joke and as a means of telling Seth that we are friends for the time being.

"Dig it," Seth says, and turns up the Odd Future track that he is playing via his iPod in the car's music system. "We be bangin'!" he says as the music shakes the vehicle's chassis. I roll up the passenger-side window lest Earl's lyrics offend someone on the street, I'm very sensitive to the feelings of strangers. Then Seth says something about where he got the system, how it was custom or something, a significant feature that you can't get off the lot, and if I want it it's an add-on, an extra One Large, because it's removable and imminently salable, but I don't even listen to him. We drive down Eighth and he turns the music off and when we stop at a light he looks over at me.

"Are you OK?" he asks again.

"What do you mean?"

"Nothing, just, you don't look so hot, man."

"I almost puked in the Starbucks if that's what you mean."

"Just now?" he asks.

"Yep," I say, "ten minutes ago."

"Cool," he says. "Why?"

I don't answer and he says I need to get laid more is my fucking problem. I need to use my bone more. I needs to be bangin' my hos more. Of course he doesn't know anything about Intern and so I don't bring her up. I let him tell me a lame story about how he's been seeing this girl that lives in his building, she sells macramé unicorns on Etsy or something, she came over one night and asked him to turn his music down, and he invited her in for a drink, and she said no, but the next night he turned his music up again really loud and she came back, this time with a joint, and they smoked it and drank some beer and then they had sex.

"That's awesome," I say. "You are totally my hero."

We pull over around Union Square and change places in the car and I drive. The Range Rover cruises quite smoothly and has plenty of pickup, which you would expect from an $85,000 automobile. I've already decided to buy it so this isn't in any way a test outing. For fun I pretend that I haven't driven in so long I can barely remember how; I screech to a stop a couple of times just inches from whatever car or person happens to be in front of me, forcing Seth to put his hand against the dashboard.

"Easy, dog," he says. "Easy on the brakes, they're Brembo and they're drilled."

Crossing east along Delancey and over the Williamsburg Bridge into my hood I suggest to Seth that we get a cocktail at the Hotel del Homo, on Berry Street on the North Side. It isn't a gay bar, but that's what I call it, because the cocktails are ridiculously bespoke.

"I'll pay," I say in response to Seth's scrunching up his face, because I know the place is not cheap. When we get to the bar it's the middle of the afternoon and so almost no one is inside, just a couple of pose-afarians writing in Middle English in their Moleskine notebooks with fountain pens. I order a bottle of a champagnelike drink to celebrate our big car-purchasing JV, and a couple of glasses into it I take out my checkbook and write Seth a check for thirty grand, which is the amount we decided on, plus the one-hundred-dollar delivery fee, less the cocktails. I don't bargain at all with him, that was the price I had floated out there initially, and if I change my mind I can always stop payment on the check, as at that point I will have his car ensconced in my building's garage and he would have nothing but a worthless piece of paper in his henna-wrought hand. It was probably quite dumb of Seth to sell me a basically new car at such a discount, but he so badly wanted to be my friend, and I don't know yet if I really want the car so we'll see. I'm thinking of it like a car I would acquire in Second Life, it doesn't really matter one way or the other, it's like a quantum cat particle at this point, poised and shimmering between being real and not having ever existed, even in jest. As we are drinking our second bottle of Cava I bring up the idea of his getting into the advertising business, which I know is the moment he's been waiting for. I can really see him salivate now, he's like a puppy and I have a fake bone that I am dangling in front of him, and he is playing it cool because he's seen me dangle it and then withdraw it before.

"No worries, but that would be so awesome," he says. "Don't I need a portfolio or something?"

"No, dude, chill, I'll get you in there," I say, speaking his language at long last. "But here's the thing, dog, you have to do me a favor first."

"Talk to me," he says, leaning forward.

"I'm in this kind of situation and I need some help getting out of it."

"Shoot, son, anything at all, I'm there for you, you know that," says the Seth. And then I tell him the story of Intern, how she was stalking me, black-hatting my e-mail, hitting on me when I was drunk and defenseless, causing herself to have a black eye and telling everyone I was the one who did it to her, while also implying that her father's attorney would be lobbing a call into the firm's general counsel, whose name is Barry, who is a walking one-man reason why feminism was invented.

"What do you want me to do?" he asks, big-eyed.

"I want you and your two friends, Titmouse and Pain, or whatever their names are, to go and pay her a visit, nothing too scary, just tell her that if she doesn't recant this black eye bullshit there will be some real, actual trouble in her vicinity."

Seth sits there and looks at me for a long time and then he says, "Dude, I dunno." He doesn't yet get that I am only fucking with him, and so I say, "What don't you know?"

"Well, I don't know if that's cool is all."

"What, you think it's cool for her to stalk me and try to get me wrapped up in some kind of human resources nightmare? Do you? You think it's cool that she gets me fired just as I'm about to bring you on board?" My voice has enough edge that now he backs off, sets his fluted flute down as if to say, I ain't drinking your booze no more, yo.

"Are you fucking with me, Eric?"

For a moment I consider laughing and slapping him on the back, filling up his glass and ordering another bottle and then the real friendship can begin, he and I, close enough to kid each other in a serious manner about something of no importance. But I want to keep the whole game alive.

"I just bought your piece of shit automobile for more than the Blue Book, asshole, and I offered you a fucking job even though the only sentences you're capable of writing are all cribbed from Peter Handke," I say now, pausing to give him time to be impressed with my highbrow lit references before continuing, "so why would I fuck with you? Why? You're like my best friend."

He melts at this, a little bit, but I can see he still has some second thoughts. "I dunno, man," he says again.

"I'm not saying you do anything illegal," I say, "I'm saying you just make certain things clear to her."

"Me?"

"Yes, you, why not? Those two hip-hop poseurs aren't going to do it. They're pussies."

"Like what do you want me to do?"

"Like I dunno you have an affadavit with you that says she caused the black eye herself and that I never touched her except in the act of sexual congress, something like that, and you get her to sign it. And Titmouse and P-Dog are your friends who come along for the ride, they provide a presence."

"And what if she refuses to sign?"

"She'll get the general drift. And if things get rough, make sure you shoot everything with your phone so there's evidence."

He says nothing. Then: "Where does she live?"

I tell him I don't know but I can get it from the office. "Cool," he says. "You don't even know her name?"

"Not really," I say. "We just hang out from time to time."

"Sweet," he says.

By this time we are finishing our third bottle, a Sardinian prosecco now, and then a minute later I'm migrating us to shots of tequila, and the place is filling up with an early evening crowd; anywhere else I'd call it a postwork crowd but not around here, the scribbling of a few lines of poetry and a half-baked idea for a Kickstarter hardly qualifying as work. A couple of young girls, pretty, excruciatingly so, are sitting in the banquette next to ours and looking at photos in their mobile devices; the one with the straight hair I think may have been in this band Au Revoir Simone, who I saw play once at Secret Monster Island Robot Basement back before it became a Whole Foods, back when it was "kewl." I can tell Seth likes them because he keeps looking over at them longingly, and he wants to impress them so I start talking, a little too loudly, about Seth's exploits as an avant garde theater director, about the piece he did in the bra factory in Long Island City, which referenced the history of Times Square topless bars, and the awesomeness of breasts, but I don't think they give a shit.

"Can I ask you guys a question?" I finally say.

"Um, OK, sorry?" the curly headed one says. She's wearing what looks like an Alexander McQueen jacket, she's well brought up and I'm willing to guess by her overall look, a lack of youthfulness in someone so young, and her expensive taste, that she was raised on the Upper East Side, went to Dalton or possibly Brearley, college at Sarah Lawrence or Smith, and now judging by the Triple Canopy totebag she works for some kind of an art-related foundation like Dia, or Soros, she doles out tidbits of money to people who make documentaries about how bad things are in faraway lands made worse by Goldman Sachs, where her dad spent twenty-five years raking it in.

"See that vehicle out there?" I ask her, pointing out of the lightly frosted glass faux-French café window to Seth's Range Rover. "I'm thinking of buying it from my friend here and, what I want to know is, just looking at him, an overall first impression, would you buy a used car from this man?"

Now the girls are with me because an actual purchase is taking place, there's shopping going on at a high level, but also this is a quick little nothing that has no consequences, it's like the conversational equivalent of an app. Seth is eating up the attention, too, they're looking him up and down now, and he's trying his best to look trustworthy, but the thing is he dresses like a fucking homeless person from the '90s, he's all worn-out hoodie and baggy jeans, what century is this, and he has his dreadlocks pulled back and a scarf on top. Both the girls shake their heads and say, "No, I don't think I would!" kind of as a joke, but also because they mean it, and then I tell them that it's too late I already wrote the check. They make some kind of comment about how I could always SMS my bank and have them cancel it, and no they don't want to go for a drive with us to the Lower East Side, or down to Dressler for the *moules frites*, they are meeting some friends later, that's so sweet but thanks.

For the rest of the night Seth and I drink, eat chorizo on a slab of old knotty wood, do a line or two in the bathroom, and as Tote Bag and her friend leave I watch while the Yoga Doctor hits on pretty much every remaining chick in the place to no avail. He really has no style at all, or rather, his style is pure old school, part white-boy rapper and part tree-hugging stoner; it's really revolting to have to watch him, looking like some refugee from a rained-out Burning Man, so I sit there and do shit on my phone, and watch the carnage pile up, as one girl after another politely turns away from him after a few moments of conversation. Finally I can't take the heartache anymore, it's too depressing, and I tell him we have to go, I have to put an end to this misery, this misery around me, the misery of perfectly turned-out young women living off their globalized daddies' fake credit boon, the misery of not seeing this as misery at all, of thinking misery exists only elsewhere, *ailleurs* as Baudelaire would say if he were here and in a way he is, always; I wonder if he looks down on his creation, this fake bohemia, with pride or contempt, and if they pay him royalties.

We get out to the street and I say I am far too wasted to drive at this point, and it's true, although I've driven in worse shape before. Seth thinks we should leave the car where we parked it and take a cab and get it in the morning. I convince him that this is a bad idea because of alternate-side parking, and he'll be fine just driving me home, it's not far, don't be a fag. We get in the car and Seth is having a hard time getting the key fob into the orifice because he's even drunker than I am. I pretend to be pissed at him, and get out of the car and start walking south on Wythe. I hear the car start up and when I look over, he has pulled up next to me.

"Get in," he says, "you're my bitch now," which doesn't even make sense. I get in without comment and he manages to get me down to Krave in one piece, it's a straight shot with red lights, we do no talking, he drives at a crawl and pulls up in front and turns off the car.

"What are you doing?" I ask him.

"It's your car now," he says, "don't you want to park it here?"

"No," I say.

"Why not? I'll get you the title tomorrow."

"Because I don't want your fucking car," I say, playing pissed off at him for about the third time tonight, as I open the door. "I drove it and it's a piece of shit vehicle."

"Eric, dude, are you crazy?"

I laugh.

"Man, you are so gullible," I say. "You're so earnest. It's good, it's cool, don't go changin'." Then I walk off toward my building. The night doorman clicks me in and I go toward the elevators without looking back. When I get up to my loftlike abode I open my sliding door and lean out onto the little balcony and look down at Kent Avenue. The RR is still there and I think that Seth has fallen asleep in it and I assume he'll stay there like that all night. But then I see the lights come on and the Rover starts up and he lurches away into the night, mad I can tell, and far too drunk to drive all the way home to Bushwick, but doing it anyway out of sheer will. I vow at that minute to block the check first thing tomorrow and then, looking at the skyline of Manhattan, I vomit over the rail and onto the grass twenty-three floors below.

My loft is white and the furniture is white, even the floors are white. I have custom white cabinets that contain a few books and some DVDs that I will throw away soon because I'm putting everything on a server, and there's an Albert Collection white sectional and a matching Albert Right-Facing Chaise, in front of them a white Eva Zeisel coffee table with an inch-thick glass top. (I ordered it custom because I felt the three-quarter-inch standard glass top was too thin for the base, it just looked wrong.) I also have a Sony Bravia KDL-70XBR3 seventy-inch flat-screen television on one of the walls, and some white lilies in a glass vase next to a Vitra Miniature Kuramata How High the Moon chair, and that little metal chair and the flat-screen are the only non-white things. Of course in the dark, the space isn't really white per se, but some light filters in at night, from the street, and from the ajarish bathroom door, because I always leave a light on in the bathroom, and so anyway at night the main room is infected with a kind of pathetic ochre wash, enough to see and move through without having to turn on an overhead. I hate overheads.

After Seth drives off, the car moving "erratically" I think out toward Bushwick, I go into the main bathroom, not the "powder room" half bath next to the kitchen, and throw up again into the sink, then I turn on the faucet and let the water run and I walk out. Much better, I think, I've purged now. I like the sound of running water, it calms me, but isn't that the most naturally calming sound in the world? I am not so unique, after all, as I would like to lead myself to believe, and even that thought isn't very original. I then take twelve Tylenol PMs because all the Ambien is gone and I go to my bed and lie down and actually sleep.

About two hours later I am jolted up but I don't know why. The pills must have kicked in enough for me to fall asleep, but now, strangely, I'm wide awake when I should be completely groggy if not fully under. Was I dreaming? Of what? Who? I get up, daylight is just breaking outside, and I check my e-mail. There's only one, it's from HR Lady, no text in the body, just a subject header that says "Google yourself."

The top hit if you Google me has always been an article in *Advertising Age* from a couple of years ago; there are other Eric Nyes in the world, of course, but for quite a while now I come up first when you get to the N. But now I type in Eric N and the *Ad Age* article comes up second; the topmost hit is Wikipedia. I wonder if there isn't a more famous Eric Nye somewhere else in the world, an Eric Nye worthy of his own Wiki entry. There were seventy-seven Eric Nyes the last time I checked on Facebook, and Google returns 3,312 results for "eric nye"; it's not the most uncommon name on the planet. Most of the matches are for me, mentions of me in relation to various awards shows or articles in advertising publications, there's an Eric Nye who is a motocross champion, and an Eric Nye who went to Columbia University. I have never met these Eric Nyes nor do I plan to.

But when I click on the link I see that this is not the Wikipedia page for Eric Nye the motocross champ, it is the Wiki page for Eric Nye the advertising creative director, aka myself. The first thing I notice is my picture. It's the sort-of official portrait of me that the agency uses for press releases, and it's all over the web, so whoever made the page could have gotten it anywhere. I'm sitting on a fancy red couch in front of a wall spray-painted in fake grafitti; you might think I am somewhere in Bed Stuy, or down by the Navy Yard, or in Red Hook, but actually I am in the agency. One of the hip young art directors who I hired is a pretty decent street artist and he did it for us; it says TATE FORWARD™! in angular fat letters, and the building management complained about the paint smell for weeks.

Eric Nye

From Wikipedia, the free encyclopedia

(redirected from "dirtbag")

Jump to: navigation, search

This article needs additional citations for verification.
Please help improve this article by adding reliable

Eric Nye (b. August 13, 1978, Canfield, Ohio) is a world-famous advertising creative director known for his award-winning work on Nike, Tide, Bank of America, and Subaru. He is currently the Chief Idea Officer at the New York office of Tate Worldwide, Inc. Tate has offices in 58 countries and their New York office is the flagship. While on his watch at Tate in less than two years, Nye has overseen a client roster that has dwindled from more than $650 million to less than $400 million in billings, marked by the departure of longtime Tate clients Tide, Bank of America, Southwest Airlines, 7UP and JC Penney.

Early Career

Eric began his career as a junior copywriter in the San Francisco office of the renowned agency Goodby, Silverstein & Partners. At Goodby he was known to work well into the night and every single weekend. He was also known for his overall malignancy, including backstabbing, asskissing, stealing ideas and taking credit for them, and running every account he's ever been on into the ground. He was fired after one year at Goodby and then was offered a job at the famed Wieden + Kennedy agency in Portland, Oregon, where he worked on the Nike golf account. While on Nike he managed to get his name attached to a multi-award-winning spot, "Saviour," directed by Spike Jonze, even though the idea was completely his art director's, who he repeatedly tried to throw under the bus to his bosses, saying that she had a questionable work ethic because she refused to come in every weekend, even though the woman had just had her first child. When the Nike clients left the agency, after nearly two decades, citing a dislike of Nye's arrogance, W+K fired him.

Nye then moved to the Netherlands, where his wealthy father supported him for a year as he tried to write a novel, which he abandoned after 20 pages, finally taking a job at boutique agency 180 Amsterdam. While at 180 his shameless, abject sycophancy in regards to the company's president/CEO was so obvious that he was hated by every person in the shop; this being advertising, the firm had no choice but to promote him. His work won awards at Cannes and D&AD in the UK, and four years later when the CCO left under mysterious circumstances, Nye was given the top job, staying on only 6 months and then leaving for Abbott Mead Vickers BBDO in London, days before 180 finally imploded.

As ECD at AMV Nye routinely appeared in the pages of *Campaign* magazine pontificating about the death of the television spot, and when three of his four global accounts jumped ship, he was quietly asked to resign, although in the press it was stated that he had left in order to move to Los Angeles because he had been taken on as a commercial director by MJZ; the latter claim was completely false. Nye lived in LA for two months, attempting to try his hand as a screenwriter, but tweeted that he had writer's block and didn't produce a single word. He was then hired to head up the creative department at Tate, where he is presently, until senior management wakes up and realizes that he has tanked every agency he's ever worked at, including this one, and he's toxic.

Family life
Nye's father, Eric Nye, Sr., inherited a firm called Amalgamated Solenoid from his father, Tony Nye (Niallo); AS manufactured small parts for the auto industry and Nye, Sr., sold the company for $5 million in 2002, but lost all his money in 2008.

Friends
Nye has no friends.

My first thought is that the entry is astoundingly accurate and must have been posted by someone who I knew pretty well, and fired, someone who would have had a grudge, but the phrase "this one," in reference to "every agency he's ever worked at," throws me off. *This* one? Wouldn't they say *"that* one"? Or "Tate"? It feels like a slip, they always give themselves away, don't they, the Criminal Class; it could be almost anyone at the agency, I know I am not well-liked. That said, I find the Wiki amusing in its own way, and assuming Tan can help me figure out who wrote it, I will call him or her in and promote them. If it was done by someone I sacked, Henry perhaps, or Juliette, I could hire them back on a freelance basis at least. Of course it could also be a good-natured joke, but since most of it is true, too true, that leaves out the one or two people at the agency with whom I have a friendly relationship, such as Tom Bridge, who would put up a bullshit Wiki on me as a goof but he's too lazy to get his facts right. Then there's her. But it can't be her, she would have no way of knowing that much about me, especially the details about my father's business and the fact that, as a first-generation Italian-American, he changed his surname, Niallo, to Nye. In fact, no one knows that much about me or my career except perhaps for my headhunter, Lynette, and she loves me or at least views me as a potential commission at some point down the line.

I click on the "history" tab at the top of the web page and there I learn that the person who wrote the bio is not a registered Wiki editor and thus their IP address is made public; in this case they were posting from a computer with the designation 191.126.92.420. I copy that number into my clipboard and send it immediately to Tan at the office. I don't include the Wikipedia URL; why risk having this sent around the gagasphere? Of course it's barely 6 AM and so he won't be able to deal with this for some time, but it's possible that before I get on the plane for LA I'll know who was stupid enough or brilliant enough to write this.

Then I decide it would be best to get some more sleep; I don't like flying much, especially when I feel guilty for drinking in public with my breakfast, but that's something I'm going to have to live with because my flight leaves at 9 AM. As I go to turn off the iMac my phone rings; it's Tan calling from his cell.

"You're up early" I say.

"Online," he says. "Multiplayer RPG with some assholes in Tokyo, Kenji Do Brian Joey Rat, and one other person, his name his name his name . . ." Tan gets stuck like a dusty CD and I have to give him a bump.

"Tan," I say, "you're breaking up."

"You hear me now?" he says, "These crazy Japanese mother-fuckers have a different time zone, keep me up all night they crazy these motherfuckers!"

"Cool," I say. "I can hear you now."

"So I get your e-mail, it's not one of ours, they all 'dot ninety-threes,'" he says.

"Meaning?"

"Meaning no problem let me get my laptop and log onto the admin server I see if I can locate."

I sit there while he does what he said he was doing. I tell him, by way of explanation, that someone using that particular computer posted something on the Internet that was potentially embarrassing for the company and I want to know who did it. He says "Oh yes that is not good!" and then I can hear him keystroking and repeating the numbers over and over as if he is memorizing them.

"One-ninety-one dot one-twenty-six dot ninety-two dot four-twenty . . ." he says to himself three or four times. Then he stops, says, "huh."

"What does that mean, 'huh'?"

"It mean, this not your IP," he says.

"No, of course not," I say.

"Where you get this?"

I figure I might as well tell him. "Wikipedia."

"I thought so," he says.

"Someone posted something and I want to know who did it."

"Two possibility," he says.

"And they are?"

"One, your home machine, not fixed IP, could be iteration."

"Meaning?"

"Meaning you do it yourself?"

"Not possible," I say. "Not possible."

"OK then two, no idea."

"What do you mean?"

"This IP not showing up, could be masked, and there two to the thirty-two power unique address on the planet," he explains.

"Is that a lot?" I ask.

There is a pause and he says, "Four billion two hundred and ninety-four million nine hundred and sixty-seven thousand two hundred and ninety-six."

"OK," I say. "That's a lot."

"Yes, that's a lot. Could be anyone, anywhere, no way to know."

"No way to know," I repeat.

"No way to know," he says. "Although likeliest story?"

"I did it myself."

"You do it to yourself."

I spend the next nearly two hours packing, taking things in and out of my Rimowa Topas aluminum suitcase, I can't decide if I should bring my Varvatos suit, my G-Star RAW belted suit jacket with the eyelets and the matching Hugo pants, or the Tom Ford, or all of them, which seems a little indecisive. I lay them into the trolley one by one and take them out one by one and I do this for a time, wondering how it is that Intern got into my apartment and posted the Wiki page without me knowing it. Actually, there are two questions unanswered: the first is when she did it and the second is how she gleaned all this info about me. Some of the basic job stuff could probably have been gotten from various articles about me in *AdWeek* or *AdAge*, but how she could have known that the idea for "Saviour" was Veronica's, or that I talked her down to senior W+K management after she had her kid, or that I only wrote twenty, exactly twenty, pages of my novel, I don't understand. I've never told anyone these things. But then I wonder, did I spill all this to her during our last encounter? Was I that high? No, I don't think I would have confided in her, why would I, it would be completely unlike me to say anything negative about myself, I'm not falsely self-deprecating like, say, Seth, am I? But is there something about Sibi, Sivi, Sari, something so disarming about her that I got super high and just poured my guts to her? Every self-loathing detail of my life? Impossible. I don't even believe in the opening up of the soul, the interior, it's all just bullshit, fashion statements for the bored; we can't ever really know ourselves, the journey inward is just more narcissism and you can't let go of the ego using the ego in defense of ego.

I look at my desk and at my iMac for some sign that someone else has used it; I don't know what such a sign would be, and it's a ridiculous impulse, and not only is it absurd but I do it twice. I pick up my mouse twice and look under it. I move my mouse pad to see if it is where I usually leave it, I move it back to where it was, then I move it again. Then I walk slowly around my loftlike apartment, looking for the telltale signs of an intruder; since there is virtually nothing in the place it would be obvious if any single piece of it had been moved. What am I looking for, some trace of nothing, an outline of two-day-old dust on a perfect white lacquer desktop? No, my cleaning lady comes twice a week, the windows are never open, there is no such thing as dust. Then I take the elevator downstairs a few minutes before my car is to arrive; I look out onto the street and it's started to rain and the car isn't there yet.

At the front desk is a short guy I haven't seen before. I ask him where the regular guy is, he says "Which regular guy? Janusz? Or Paolo?" I never learned the regular guy's name, the guy who is here in the evenings mostly, in his little black jacket and bow tie, with the logo of the management company, Superior Management, on the pocket (possible tagline: THE NAME IS SO UNORIGINAL IT HAS TO BE GOOD™) but since my memory of the regular guy is that he is skinny and blond I guess it would be Janusz.

"He quit," short guy says. So I ask him if there's any way he could look and see if someone was let into my apartment while I wasn't here.

"You mean we let them in with a key?" he's asking me.

"Yes."

He gets onto his computer and does some typing and mousing around. "What is your number, sir, please?"

"Twenty-three *F*."

"Superior Cleaning Services, Monday and Thursday."

"Nothing else?"

"No." I hear a car honking outside and it's my limo so I go out. The rain has started to fall harder now and I am getting in the car when I realize that I have left my Romowa trolley in the lobby. Funny, I think, all that consternation about the packing and what if I just left it there and had to buy all new clothes on Melrose? I go back in and it's sitting there, bright red and yellow metal, inert, like R2-D2's battery went dead. As I retrieve it the short guy is still looking at the computer.

"Wait a moment one second," he says in an accent that is either Italian or Czech. "It say here we let you in because you forget your key."

"Me?" I ask.

"Yes, you come in and you forget your key and we let you in. Yes, it was Janusz do it. Before he quit and move back to Gdansk."

"When?"

"He leave today."

"No, when did he let me in?"

"Yesterday ago."

In the limo riding out Grand Central Parkway to JFK we get on the Jackie Robinson Parkway, which roars through what's left of a forest, a forest where they shot the original silent Tarzan movies before the movie business moved itself out to the west coast. Of course I have no memory of having left my key in my apartment and being let in by Janusz or anybody else because that never happened. On the other hand, two days ago was when I last saw Intern, maybe it was when we were coming back from the bar, shitfaced off our asses, stumbling in, that was the night she bumped her head on the door jamb, I can almost imagine that we were so drunk I don't remember having Janusz let us in, and the log would not record that there were two of us, and two days back is what he meant by yesterday ago? It doesn't make sense. It's possible I was with her, but at the very least I'm sure I would have remembered the feeling of being mortified to be seen dragging a teenager home with me in full view of a judgmental Pole or Ecuadorian or whoever else was representing Superior Management that night. And what about Janusz's disappearance? Why did he quit and move back to the motherland, anyway? Maybe I don't remember him letting me in because in fact he never did let me in, he let someone else in, perhaps a girl, somewhat reminiscent of a Photoshopped Chantal Goya, who no doubt performed favors in exchange for the favor, and then she went nuts on him, too, and so he got fired for being deemed Inferior Management and decided to leave town. It's also possible if not much more likely that how it was done and by whom is simply not something I will ever know; with this knowledge I arrive at my terminal, swipe the driver, and go inside.

The check-in at the airport is perfectly smooth, as it almost always is in first class, and I wait at the gate, pretending to look at my phone but really just staring at the bulge in my pants caused by the erection that my meds won't let subside. I have to admit that Barry is no dummy, he gets it, I don't have to worry about Barry. There was a problem, a problem with the kid, Barry is telling his old boss on the phone from Boca, the asshole doesn't know how to keep his dick in his trow, so I, Barry, I had to handle it, I had to have a talk with him, I had to tell him how to manage his own inaccuracies, no that's not the word, his own, what is the word, inadequacies, no, his own incontinence, oh fuck it, how's the buffet at the club?

I realize since I'm thirsty I should have gone to the first-class lounge but I didn't, I hate those places, I don't know why, with the exception of the Virgin Clubhouse, and so I go to the food court. There's a McDonalds, a Chipotle, a Sakkio Japan, a California Pizza Kitchen, a P.F. Chang's China Bistro, a Boston Chowda, a Cold Stone Creamery, and a Dunkin' Donuts. I choose the California Pizza Kitchen because it has the shortest line but when I get there a family sneaks in front of me, rendering that decision invalid, and so I move over to the Dunkin' Donuts area, which has a large open cooler filled with beverages. I stand in front of it and choose a drink. Just as I'm reaching for a SmartWater a guy there informs me that the ones in the bottom row are warm, they were just put in and the kid didn't even bother to move them to the back where they could get cold, he just put them right in front, but the ones at the top, on the right side, are really cold, here, he says, feel this one, and he takes a SmartWater down and hands it to me. I take it from him and indeed it is cold to the touch.

"Thanks," I say, and he nods, smiles, and moves off. Obviously he's not from New York, he's probably from the Midwest, from my home state of Ohio perhaps, who believes it's acceptable to offer help to strangers. I go back to the gate and drink the water, or half of it, and then they announce that my flight is boarding. I get up and grab my Booq laptop bag and head onto the plane. I get my seat, 3A, and settle in for the flight. I down my first champagne quickly and the attendant fills me up again right away. I down that one too and she gives me a smile and a refill and some warm nuts in a small white bowl. I don't eat the nuts. Why don't I eat the nuts? Then a moment later she swoops in, I'm hoping to give me another glass of cheap cru, but instead she takes the nuts away.

"There's someone on the plane who's allergic," she explains in an almost-whisper. "All the nuts have to go."

As I said, I don't like to fly; it has nothing to do with the thought that the plane might go down, I've many times wished for such an end, it would be, I should think, completely pain-less, or at worse a few nanomoments of pain, and it would cer-tainly be an exciting experience to have, a real adrenaline rush as you plummeted, and there would be no shame in it, it would not be like getting in a car accident where you were at least partly at fault, especially if you were drunk, and it wouldn't be like, say, getting killed in a bank robbery where someone could say, after your death, "What was he doing at a branch so far from his home?"

During takeoff I listen to the new Best Coast tracks that our music department gave me, they haven't even been released yet, and I was promised this band was really going to blow up, which no doubt they will, as their music is really awful, asinine, and cloying. Once we are airborne I fall asleep. I dream that I am in the Tate office and someone, I don't know who, I don't think they even have a face, I'm not even sure if they are male or female, is running up and down the halls with a gun kill-ing people, just randomly sticking a Glock or some other kind of handgun into cubicles and offices and blowing people away. There's a lot of blood. But there's no sound, so the overall effect isn't all that different from a regular day at work.

When I wake a few hours later, the pilot is making an an-nouncement: we are passing over the Rocky Mountains and there might be some turbulence, please fasten your seatbelts.

That's when I realize I'm not breathing normally, I'm breathing in quick, short gasps, and my lips are dry and chapped, I must have been sucking in air through my mouth as I slept. This isn't unusual, I oftentimes wake with chapped lips, and I have to wipe the pasty stuff off on a towel in the bathroom, or sometimes I use a paper towel in the kitchen, but the irregularity of my breathing is what's troubling me, not the gunk.

I look around as the plane begins bouncing on some rough air, "chops" is I think what they call it, and I note that my breathing issues preceded said choppiness, so it isn't that I'm concerned about a crash, all of us stuck in a blizzard for weeks and eating one another, no, the panic is about something else: there, I said it, here we go again, is this the big one? The first thing that comes to mind is I'm reacting to the dream I had, which I know was fairly violent and scary, but it's difficult to know if it was a dream about some kind of subconcious fear of retribution on the part of someone I've let go, or if the faceless killer is in fact me carrying out my gruesome task. But either way, my feeling tone about the dream isn't all that negative so I don't think that's what is making it hard, harder now, to take in air, to breathe, and guess what, it's getting worse.

The other possibility is that I'm allergic to nuts? I've heard of sympathetic toxic reactions, some kind of Nut Allergy by Proxy, but I didn't even eat them (warm almonds, cashews, peanuts), I barely even looked at them before they were jerked away. I start to glance around the plane, it's quiet except for the turbulence, but everyone is in their seat and we're letting it pass, a brief section of gustiness over the hills, and after a couple of minutes of me trying to take long, deep breaths in order to even things out, I know it's a losing battle. Here we go again and to make matters worse I left my Klonopin in my trolley.

I have to get up. I have to get to the bathroom. I undo my seatbelt and stand in the aisle and move forward toward the lav, taking big wide steps to keep my balance as the plane shudders. One of the flight attendants, with a name tag that says "LUCY," is strapped to her little seat and she tells me to please sit down. I ignore her, in fact for a moment I consider flipping her the bird, and I go into the john. Once inside I sit on the toilet, on the lid of it, and hold on with my left hand to the handle, which is midway up the plastic wall. I have those thoughts of killing myself again, like I'm possessed by them, the enclosed space is not helping things, but at least I'm alone. I've often thought they put the handles on the wrong side in these lavatories, because if there's turbulence and you're trying to pee while standing up, you want the handle on the left side (which it would be if you were facing the bowl instead of sitting on it as I am now) so that you can hold your dick and aim with your right hand. But that's something that can be explained in any number of ways. First of all, not everyone is right-handed, some people hold their dicks with their left hands while peeing, probably not that many, but some. And then of course some people don't even have dicks at all because they're eunuchs or, in other cases, women. And then there's the fact that it's probably wiser to just sit while pissing on a plane anyway no matter who you are. Finally after some time the turbulence goes and I can concentrate on the feeling of irrelievable doom that has taken hold of me, a firey, deep-in-my-chest sense that all manner of terrible things are going to happen, not now, not even soon, but sometime, when is the only question. Please, please I pray this plane crashes, although I venture I am the only one on it who would benefit. At any rate I try to distance myself from this now time-unspecific sense of impendingness by giving it a name, I call it Meta-Doom and a brand color, which is black, and then I'm writing a brief for Meta-Doom in my head. *Key Message: Having an inescapable sense of Meta-Doom gives me social status among my peer group because it underscores my intelligence and creativity. Brand Character: masculine, powerful, aspirational, angry. Brand Look and Feel: Black. Dark. Brand Attitude: Grim. Brand Character: Kafka meets a Predator drone. Target Consumer: Eric Nye, male, thirty-three, a creative individualist who naturally makes unconventional choices while staying true to self.*

The lavatory on an airplane is an excellent place to write a brief in your head, I realize, or to just let your mind wander, which eventually I am able to do, trying not to pay too much attention to this wish to end my existence, keeping my mind on other things, such as how to market Meta-Doom to the planet, but how can I blame myself if I can't breathe? It feels like someone is rendering me to Rammstein with a black plastic bag over my head. And then there is the banging on the door, and the voice of the flight attendant, motherly in a way, am I alright? The plane has begun its inevitable descent into Los Angeles International Airport, aka LAX, why would they add the most ominous letter in the alphabet to the letters L and A? Unless it's to remind us all to come back, i.e., to re-LAX, be happy, and suddenly the door is opened from outside with a special key. One and a half hours is a long time to sit in a commode without even once using the thing, and it's the only one in first class, I realize I must have inconvenienced my fellow passengers, and now the flight attendant has busted in.

"Are you OK?" she is asking me.

"I had some kind of attack," I tell her.

"An attack?" she says.

"I guess you would call it a Meta-Doom Attack."

Everyone knows what that is, she nods, asks me if I am alright, do I need medical assistance, and so on. I'm guessing she is required to say these things for insurance purposes.

"We were knocking and knocking, I finally had to come in."

"No worries," I tell her politely. But then she looks into the lav and sees, to her sudden surprise, that someone has haltingly scrawled sentences, in English, on the beige plastic walls with a black felt-tip pen. I look back in and see what she sees: nonsense phrases written all over, I'm surprised I didn't notice them earlier.

SO MUCH BETTER THAN THE OLD TIMES.™
LOOK UP IF YOU WANT TO GET DOWN.™
THAT'S THE FEELING YOU'LL GET, TODAY, ALL
    DAY.™
SEE IT OUR WAY, AND YOU'LL KNOW THE POWER
    OF META-DOOM.™
JUST BE YOURSELF, THE REST WILL FOLLOW.™
    (MATTRESS)

Immediately I recognize two things: one, that these are taglines and, two, that they are in my handwriting; it's true I often have a Sharpie in my jacket pocket for the times when I have an idea and don't want to type it into my phone.

"Did you do this?" she asks me. "Did you write this?"

"I may have," I say, "I mean, that may be my handwriting."

"May be?"

"I guess it is my handwriting."

Why I admitted this I'm not sure. I could have said someone else did it. She looks at me with, for a moment, an intense curiosity, as if she could see through me, like I am just a diorama in a medical museum.

"I'm going to have to fill out a report."

"OK, if you must."

"In the meantime there are other passengers that would like to use the lavatory."

I go back to my seat, avoiding any eyes that are looking my way, and buckle up for landing. When we reach the gate and the door is opened, a Los Angeles Port Authority officer, white, forties, with a mustache, comes on before anyone can get off. The attendant points at me and he comes to my row. He asks me if I will accompany him off the plane, they have some questions for me. I don't argue with him, why would I? He takes me to a Port Authority office, it's way at the end of the terminal, we walk there in total silence, mustache cop and another cop, also in uniform, he's black and about my age. As we get to the office, the three of us, white cop leading the way and black cop right behind me to make sure I don't make a run for it, the brains and the brawn of law enforcement as it were, and I'm thinking if this were a TV show it would be reversed, the networks are sensitive to claims of racial stereotyping. They sit me down in a light blue room and ask me why it is I did what I did. I can't come up with an answer and then they have me sign some kind of paper saying I will pay for the damages to the airplane, which of course I sign readily, saying that I abhor what I did, which is true, I don't even like so-called street art, even Banksy, I hate Banksy, he's a phony, it's just vandalism in my book whether it's on the side of an abandoned building or at the New Museum. Then they let me go. I go to baggage claim and my Rimowa is waiting for me; I wheel it into a bathroom and get the Klonopin and down a handful and wait, wait, for the edge to burn off.

I look at myself in one of the big mirrors in the bathroom—my face clean-shaven, my hair cascading over my ears—and I can't believe my eyes, I am waiting for the drugs to do their thing. Is that me in there? And then, like ghosts, like nearly forgotten memes, the half-opaque faces of the fallen surround me in the glass: Henry, Dave and Bob, Gayle, Beatrice, George, Nan, Jay, Justin, Jordon, Sam, Harlan, Cyril, Kevin, Mike, and so many more, all at 50 percent opacity, looking back at me, at my face, loosed of any bodily anchor. And then Juliette, in the middle of them, staring at me, her mascara making a horror show of her face. What a world, what a world, I hear myself saying to the room, who would have thought someone so young and weak could destroy my beautiful wickedness? I look at my reflection again and it's as clear as night: I'm falling into the abyss, I'm done.

Then I go back into baggage claim and out the sliding doors. The weather in LA is a predictable seventy-six degrees and it's sunny and for a moment I think I can smell burning eucalyptus in the air.

part three

"My mother killed herself" is a phrase I have written, thought, thought out loud, said out loud, said to myself, written by hand, typed, shouted, and yet it still isn't true no matter how many times I repeat it. Yes, it's true she went mad, it's true she died by her own hand, but still "killed herself" somehow doesn't tell the story, or at least tell it accurately enough. There were mitigating factors, as there always are, and perhaps from far off "suicide" is a word that describes a particular action, said action being sufficient to warrant certain explanations for behavior and attitude, and I have been guilty in the past of exploiting the event and turning it into a master narrative and this is what in the end makes it at least partly false. I'm thinking this as I stand there waiting for the Avis bus and then at once I change my mind, decide not to rent a car. Maybe it was the experience of being in Seth's Range Rover, or the sight of him wandering off into the night in it, from my window, perhaps to his demise, a crash on the BQE I imagine, or at least him getting pulled over and having his license taken away and the car impounded, or was it my mental state, which teetered on the edge of utter oblivion: At any rate driving seeming like a bad idea then and it does now. I take a cab to the hotel. On the way up Lincoln Boulevard there's an ambulance blocking traffic and it looks like a hairy, wild-eyed man has chained himself to a shopping cart; they are trying to cut the chain with a bolt cutter, to free him in order to take him to jail. When we get past the ambulance, traffic moves again. We wait through two greens at the left onto Pico but then we get the arrow and sail west toward the sea.

Shutters on the Beach is in Santa Monica, on the water as the name implies, and it's always where I stay in LA; in fact I lived here for nearly two months while I was looking for an apartment, during my so-called Hollywood screenwriting phase. Harrison Ford stayed here during that time; he was shooting a movie called *Firewall*, which had the working title *Untitled Harrison Ford Project*, I can tell you he's much older in person than he is while lit up properly, with gauze on the lens or whatever it is they do, and he brought a dog with him all the way from New York. I get my early check-in and the room I am assigned is in the back, in the new building, the one that is nestled against the hill that goes up toward Main Street, toward Capo, one of my favorite restaurants near the beach (the other is Sushi Roku), and immediately I know that this room will not do at all. For one thing, to get to it you have to walk across the pool deck area to an elevator, you have to take the elevator up a level, and then you walk across a kind of little bridge and then you have to go down some stairs, totally defeating the purpose of the elevator ride. It's as if stairs are an outdated technology so there's a useless elevator journey included free with your stay.

The next room they show me is on the floor above, and it's equally unacceptable. Most of the rooms at Shutters are done in a kind of Cape Cod beach theme, some of them more so than others, and this one immediately makes me uncomfortable; there are too many conch shells lying around, too many jade-colored light sconces, too many shawl-like blankets, too many David Halberstam books on the shelves. I force the front-desk girl, friendly, perky, thirties, obviously an aspiring actress, to let me look at a room in the main building, she says there aren't any available for the week that I will be here, but I know that isn't true, they always keep rooms open for last minute VIPs and so on, if you are willing to pay, and I am. She has Paul take me to a room with not a beach view exactly but one looking north up the coast, or rather, onto a parking lot; yes, that's more like it. I tip the guy a twenty, roll my R2-D2 trolley inside (I had left him in the hall in case this room didn't work out either), and the first thing I do in any hotel room is I turn on all the lights in the bathroom, even the heat lamp; then I sit on the edge of the bed. About three minutes later there is a knock on the door, I get up and answer it. It's another of the bellboys with a fruit basket for me; I assume it is from the production company, Gangrape, as it's de rigueur for them to lavish the agency people with little welcome gifts like this. He sets the fruit basket down on a side table and goes out. There's a small card in an envelope and I open it. The card does not have the Gangrape logo on it (a few horny rabbits wearing dildos), in fact the card has no logo at all, just three words written in girly handwriting.

"See you soon!" it says.

I toss the card into the little wicker trash bin and close all the curtains on the windows that face the parking lot and make the room as dark as possible. I try for about an hour to masturbate and don't get anywhere. It's impossible to imagine that she is in LA and sent me this fruit basket. I read the card again, I stare at it like a man looking down into a ravine from a high perch, I pick up the room phone and dial the front desk and ask if they knew who it was who sent it; the guy tells me they will check their records and get back to me. Then I call HR Lady back at the office. She doesn't pick up and I leave a message. "It's Eric. Please call me as soon as you can," I say. "Look, I know what's happening, I don't give a fuck about my bonus, I'm having a nervous breakdown, just call me, please." Then I get a little pad of Shutters on the Beach stationery and make some quick calculations. If I were to resign, my salary alone would add up to almost all the salaries of the people I've fired. Meaning that if I were to quit I could hire most of them back without increasing the payroll. The catch of course is that if I were to resign I would have no authority to hire anyone much less the people I had already fired.

The bar is closed, it's not quite 1 PM, so I go out to the pool. The light is getting brighter as the fog and pollution burn off, and I realize I should be wearing my sunglasses. But I don't want to go all the way back to the room so I go to the lobby and down the stairs to the spa, where I know they have a tiny quote-unquote "store" that sells extremely expensive beach stuff such as bespoke sunscreen, hats, Japanese sandals, and Ray-Bans. I buy the Ray-Bans and go back to the pool deck. The temperature is in the eighties already and it's climbing. I sit in a deck chair and face away from the beach; something about the ceaseless idiocy of one wave after another strikes me as profoundly unimaginative. I consider changing hotels; I could stay at the Four Seasons, which is nowhere near the beach, or even the Standard, in downtown LA, also not near the beach, but the production company we're working with, Gangrape, is fairly close, in Culver City, and since I didn't rent a car it seems like a bad idea to be so far away. I decide to wait here at the pool until Tom Bridge and the FreshIt creatives from the agency arrive.

From the pool attendant I order some shrimp kind of skewer thing and I can hear the tractors out on the beach tilling the previous day's trash into the sand; I don't feel well. The last time this happened to me I managed to comfort myself with work, so I think why not try again? I go back to my room and get my FreshIt folder; in it there is a printout of a PowerPoint document, sixty-five pages of information about the launch of the new FreshIt World of Scents scent-making device. I take the printout back to the pool. The sun is bright now, and it's hard to read. Most of the pages are white.

The first page just says FreshIt World of Scents in the Lucida Grande typeface and behind the title in the upper right-hand corner is an egglike purple and green circular whoosh that is meant to convey, I'm guessing, the excitement and energy of new technology. And that it does, beautifully. I stare at the swoosh for I don't know how long, imagining how many high-level meetings there were in the offices of the Microsoft Corporation, on the huge campus in Redmond, Washington, to discuss the heft and hue of the egglike smoosh, whether the soft focus green band on the left side was really working with the purple orbish center or not, let's explore some options for Wednesday's meeting. The second page of the PowerPoint document sets up the structure of the deck. Part One (twelve pages) is about the product itself. The product is a machine that emits a series of awful, saccharine, synthetic fragrances—Brazilian Picnic, Aloha Sky, Hibiscus Morning, Rainforest Mist, and five others. It's kind of like an electric scented candle; as such it is an obvious improvement on a real scented candle because a) FreshIt World of Scents doesn't require a dangerous household flame in order to work, the way a candle does, and b) it costs a lot more than a scented candle, because it has moving parts, thereby employing more people in China where it is manufactured, as well as using fossil fuels to generate the electricity that it runs on, so everybody wins.

The reason we are here in Los Angeles is to create a series of commercials meant to convince people to buy FreshIt World of Scents at their nearby Walmart. And that's where the remaining forty-seven pages of the PowerPoint deck come in. Part Two (twenty-four pages) gets to the meat of it, our consumer insight, or what we at Tate call the Heart-Mind-Key. The Heart-Mind-Key is a proprietary tool, developed by us to aid our clients in really getting inside the hearts and minds of our target consumer. Page 28 of the deck is entitled The FreshIt World of Scents Heart-Mind-Key Insight Driver. Bulleted half-sentences beneath the title are written in the voice of Abby. Pages 45 and 46 of the doc (Addendum B) tell us that Abby is thirty-four, married, with three children ages two to ten; she lives in the South or perhaps the Midwest. She does not presently work (she's a homemaker!) but was employed for a few years, as an administrative assistant or perhaps a schoolteacher, and she quit when her second child was born, and her family's median income is $32,000 a year. She's in touch with the latest trends, she's an Information-Seeker, she's Family-Oriented, spends four hours a week online, reads *Redbook* and *Family Circle*, votes conservative, is religious, enjoys her friends when there's time, is probably obese, has pets, several pets, that stink up the place, and is too busy as a modern mom to devote the needed thirty minutes of each day to housecleaning. Abby isn't a real person, of course, she's the creation of our new Director of Psychographics, Nigel, a gay guy from London who has a PhD in psychology from Oxford. What Nigel might presume to know about women from the Deep South, a place he's never been and wouldn't even feel safe visiting, is beyond me.

The four bulleted half-sentences in Abby's voice read:

- FWS turns my house into a home
- FWS is like my own private spa inside of my mind
- FWS is my reward for being a caring homemaker
- FWS confirms my love for my family

Immersing myself in the research works for a while but then the plastic bag is wrapped tightly around my head once more. I want to die. So I realize the best thing to do right now would be to get out of here, out of this hotel and away from this ocean with its relentless predictability, and so I throw some clothes on and head out. The bellboy who brought me the fruit basket is in the lobby, he opens the door for me with a smile.

"Basket you brought," I say to him in a wheezy desperate voice, "who give?"

"Sorry?"

"Who gave to you?"

"Sir?" he asks.

"Who give you that fruit?"

"I don't know," he says. "I believe it was another guest at the hotel that gave you that fruit basket, if that's indeed what you are referring to, a young woman."

It was impossible to consider. "Can you describe?"

"Um, young, not tall, dark hair, petite, pretty . . . very pretty . . ."

"And you say guest at hotel?"

"I believe so."

I look away, sucking in air in an attempt to keep my lungs from imploding.

"Didn't she leave a name on the card?" he asks.

"No," I say.

"Would you like me to ask at the desk, sir?"

"Just get me a fucking cab. Please." He jumps through the door and there happens to be a taxi in the circle outside that has just dropped off a guest. It's Mark Ruffalo, and I don't even wait for the driver to take his bag out of the trunk before getting in. Then the driver gets back in and looks at me.

"The nearest hospital," I tell him.

He gives me a look and then pulls out of the circular drop-off and takes a left up Pico. Fifteen minutes later we pull up at UCLA Medical Center, right in front of the emergency room. A sign says Authorized Vehicles Only and while I'm paying the driver a security guard is heading toward us to wave us off. As I lurch past him into the ER I notice he's rocking a pair of Reebok Ex-O-Fit Hi Straps.

The diagnosis is Acute Anxiety Reaction. I probably would have just been given some IV propranolol and sent on my way after an hour or two of observation, but I became extremely agitated while waiting for the doctor to look at me and I may have knocked some things over, a table perhaps, and a couple of chairs. Subsequently I had to be restrained to a bed, which is when I got the Ativan, and then I relaxed and went down for a whole two days. I must have needed the sleep. This means I've missed our preproduction meeting with the clients, I've missed our casting callbacks, I've missed our kickoff dinner with the folks from Gangrape—I think we were going to Koi. I also realize that I've left my phone at the hotel, there are probably a hundred messages inquiring where the fuck I am. I go over it in my mind, did I tell the bellhop I wanted to go to the hospital? No. There's no way that anyone would for a second suspect that this is where I am. What they figure, with good reason, is that I met a girl at a bar or on the beach and went home with her, and being a tweaker she murdered me, or I'm on some kind of bender, screwing my brains out with some jewelry designer from the desert or something. It's not a big deal. The appropriate lies will have been told the clients, I had a Family Emergency back in Ohio, his mother, he's so, so sorry not to be here, he's been weighing in on the casting, he had a long talk with the director about it, he's still very involved, this is one of his top priorities. I try to reach the nurse's call button but can't, I see there are restraints holding me tight to the bed frame. I squirm and try to loosen them but no.

I sink down into the mattress and the restraints loosen on their own; for the first time in my entire life I feel free.

For the next couple of hours I watch a reality show called *Hooker Bust*, and then another one called *Operation Repo* and another called *Party Heat* and another about fat white people who talk like they're from the ghetto and seem to exist on nothing but Red Bull. During all this I think about what I will do if I get fired and my options in advertising have winnowed. I've tried screenwriting, I've tried writing writing (i.e., fiction), I've tried poetry (high-school paper), I've tried directing (two web-only spots for Nike), maybe I need to make a bigger break, a clean break with creativity, get into something like accounting or engineering. Or I could teach. It would be really cool to be an industrial designer and design things like chairs or iced-tea glasses, or mobile devices, but that would require going back to school. Same with computer programming, same with being an entertainment lawyer, which is something I considered, same with psychiatry. These days every profession requires an advanced degree; this is most likely because globalization has reduced the need for a sizable local workforce, so graduate schools have stepped in to provide a few extra years of postcollege babysitting. For a time I had even wanted to be an architect, but I looked into it and architects make little and work long hours. Besides, there's something revolting about building houses for other people to live their lives in, enabling their addictions to magical thinking, reality television, and so on; maybe I should just stick to being a high priest in the state-mandated church of involuntary materialism. Maybe I could move to Haiti and work for Sean Penn; I knew a music video director who had met him at a lawn party in Bolinas. Before I can decide my post-advertising fate, the nurse-attendant comes and undoes my straps because I have a meeting with the doctor.

Dr. Jaktar is a nice-enough man from the Punjab region of India. He is probably forty, balding, and has thick black eyebrows that meet in the middle; I ask during the initial pleasantries if he is a Muslim and he says he was born a Muslim but converted to Catholicism when he got married. I'm gathering he may have married a nurse that he met while doing his internship in Ireland. Jaktar is a psychiatrist and he has a few questions for me; I quickly ascertain that since I am now calm and collected and the Stress Event, as he keeps calling it, whatever it was, is over, I can go. I don't tell him this, but I don't want to go just yet; going can only mean returning to Shutters on the Beach, and to the FreshIt shoot. I'm just not ready to look at eight hours of callbacks of perky middle-aged women, the so-called Abbys, shrugging to camera, smiling, winking, and saying "I love my family—even if they don't always notice all the cool things I do for them!" I just can't stomach this shit anymore, I'm experiencing a classic case of metanoia. For a moment, as I'm giving Dr. Jaktar some basic information about my medical history, I consider having another temper tantrum, maybe just reaching out and knocking his monitor from his desk with a quick jerk of my hand, or overturning his chair in a fit of sudden rage, but I don't want to repeat myself. So I finally tell him that I've been thinking of committing suicide, I've been having suicidal thoughts lately, they run in the family, and he perks up at this, this is like the holy grail for these guys, he can see his income stream widening.

"Would you say you're depressed?" he inquires.

"No."

"Have you ever been diagnosed as having depression?"

"No."

"Then how would you know what depression is?" he asks. I tell him I guess I have no idea what it is, I just know I'm not depressed, I'm highly functioning, I'm on a mission to reinvent a very large, traditional agency, and apart from a few bumps in the road such as my becoming an evil troll, it's going swimmingly.

He uncrosses a leg and leans in toward me, deeply interested. I tell him that despite my feelings of intense self-loathing, which potentially date back to my early teens, I don't want to off myself, it's been done to death, so to speak, I just think about it from time to time, it's a subject that interests me on a philosophical level, perhaps, according to Tacitus or somebody, the only question worth asking. Isn't life, after all, as some German hipster once wrote, nothing more than one long, comical, failed (and ultimately successful?) suicide attempt? I also tell him without hesitation that I am happy, that I've always been happy, ever since I was a baby, more or less, so it's confusing to me why I have so many thoughts of death but I just have them, perhaps it's only a maudlin interest of mine, the way some people are obsessed by other dark topics such as the Civil War or World War I or World War II or the Vietnam War or the Iraq War or war in general or hunting or family dynamics or serial killers or that 4chan internet meme where they Photoshop pictures of a mutilated Miley Cyrus. Then I tell him the story of sitting at the pool at Shutters and staring out at the ocean reading about people and their smelly homes in need of privatized electronic scent enhancement. "There's something undeniably sad and at the same time exalted about that, don't you think?" I ask him. "Don't you?"

"About people needing a fake scent in their homes? Or about you spending your time working to sell such a thing?"

"Both, obviously. They're the same."

"How do you mean?"

"Because they're both lies, the scent itself and our firm's representation of it in the world, and lies are a window onto the truth, something like that."

He doesn't say a thing for a time and then he tells me that they will keep me here another day for observation. He remarks that my period of agitation seems to have passed, so I will not be tied down, and he apologizes for the physical restraints but the insurance requires it, as well as the diazepam I was given as a chemical restraint, which I note is a benzodiazepine, otherwise known as a roofie: I'm being date raped! That makes me think of Intern, her behavior at certain times, as well as mine. Did she slip me something in one of those pomegranate-infused Belvedere-and-Veuve chamtinis? Did she slip something to herself and make the blood test a part of her pogrom against me?

As Jaktar goes on about scheduling an appointment with a psychotherapist for some "talking therapy" as he calls it, I read a flowchart on the wall behind him to give me something else to focus on. The flowchart tells what to do if a patient is confused. First, determine if the cause of the confusion is environmental or not. If it is, remove the cause of the confusion, then reassess. If confusion persists, medicate. I determine that the cause of my own confusion right now is Dr. Jaktar and his involuntary Punjabi head bobbing; I just want to go back to my room and watch television. There is a pause so I stand up, thinking he is dismissing me, but he doesn't move and he says, in one quick burst, "Tell me about Dr. Look."

I did not see this coming. I sit back down.

"How do you know about Dr. Look?" I ask him.

"When you were sedated we looked in your wallet to see if you had medical coverage; when you became violent you lost certain rights pertaining to your privacy. We found his business card. What can you tell me about him?"

"I don't know anything about him," I say. "Why?"

Jaktar gives me a squint that I believe is meant to indicate he thinks I'm lying. Then he says, "I attempted to contact this Dr. Look but couldn't locate him. He's not board certified in the state of New York, he's not on anybody's list of psychiatrists in the state of New York, I don't think he is practicing in the state of New York." It really bothered me how often he had said "the state of New York."

"I was referred to him by the General Counsel of our company," I said, "Barry Spinotti, who is effectively my boss since we don't have a president or CEO right now, the last one having quit. Barry referred me to Dr. Look and that's all I know about him. He has an office on Lexington Avenue. Six-eighty-six or six-sixty-eight or eighty-eight-six or something like that. In the fifties near the Citicorpse tower. He said he'd gone to Harvard."

"I've never been to New York," Jaktar admits. "Harvard you say?"

For a minute or two we talk about New York and the differences between New York and LA. I tell him I love LA and used to live here, but hated the weather; he says he has some distant cousins in Queens and should really go and see them at some point. Then he crosses his other leg and sits back in his chair and nods; the second pleasantry-based section of our conversation has just ended.

"Mr. Nye," he says, "why would the head of your company tell you to go and see a psychiatrist who doesn't exist?"

"I don't know," I say. I sense I am in some kind of a battle with Dr. Jaktar only I don't know what the rules are and I don't know what it would mean to lose. "It all seemed kind of fishy to me as well."

"In what way?"

"Well his office wasn't even a real office, it was like an old apartment that hadn't ever been renovated. It had an old kitchen in the back, and there was a couch that was so dilapidated it had been repaired with duct tape. Does that sound like a psychiatrist's office to you?"

"No," he says, "it does not."

"Exactly," I say. "Because all of this could be part of some kind of setup on the company's part to fire me without paying my bonus. It's all a lie. Which undoubtedly is what motivated me to lie to this Look character, to make up some story about my mom dying in a car accident when I was a boy."

"I'm sorry to hear that," he says. He looks at me and his expression changes; suddenly I feel we are on the same page again, we are allies in something but I don't know what. "When did she die?"

"About twenty years ago," I go. "I was a boy." I say no more. He nods.

"So what I'm curious to know is why did the people at your firm tell you to see a psychiatrist in the first place?" he then asks, and the moment of our alignment, our fleeting shared membership in the human race, is gone.

"Because there's a situation at our office, and they're trying to drive me crazy," I blurt out, immediately wondering if that was a good idea and then immediately thinking yes it was. "She's an intern, she's accused me of sexual harrassment, and it's a completely baseless claim, and Barry said he wanted me to see the shrink because he would give me a clean bill of health. It's all a scam, the whole thing. I mean if he wasn't a real shrink and only pretending to be one, that's a scam, but maybe he is a real shrink, and only pretending to be a scam artist in order to either a) rake in a little cash on the side or b) actually help people. At any rate, I think the whole thing was set up years ago by my company to help them get out of legal problems." Then I told him, at far too great a length, about the sordid history of Tate and how the Old Man, when he was running things, was the biggest ass grabber in the history of Madison Avenue, and how the company had gotten bloated over the years so it was time to get lean and mean; I had been hired to be the agent of this much-needed-correction but had recently reached what I felt was the end of my complicity.

Jaktar thinks. If he were in a graphic novel I would have scrawled HMMM . . . in the thought bubble to the left of him. He nods again, I don't even think he knows he's doing it, and then he turns toward his computer and does some typing. I try to lean over and read it but of course the whole thing, in terms of angles, conspires against me, so I see nothing.

"It's my professional opinion that you could use some rest, Eric," he says. "Don't you agree?"

All hospitals are the same, all hallways lead to nowhere, and in this one the doors are locked, making circular journeys impossible. Apart from the food, which is inedible, it's not too bad here, in fact it's quite pleasant even though I no longer qualify for the Klonopin drip, they've got me on Ativan. I watch a lot of television, trying to ignore the commercials for payday loans and fabric softener and stool softener and cars that offer to make your payments if you lose your job, and I masturbate frequently in a vain attempt to rid myself of the erection that won't stop. I also play dominos in the day room with a schizophrenic woman named Melanie who keeps shouting "WE'VE GOT SUITCASES! WE'VE GOT SUITCASES!" at the top of her lungs. I even let her win a couple of times, which makes her cry, and when she cries I hold her hand and this seems to calm her down and when she's calm she smiles. "We've got suitcases," she says quietly to no one, although for a second I think she means me.

The next day, when I get up and get dressed and sign my discharge papers and go outside, I am wearing the same Adriano Goldschmied jeans and J. Lindeberg shirt I came in with, and I decide to walk to the beach rather than take a cab; it's not that far and it's early so I'll arrive at the hotel before anyone even gets up. I'm rested and in a good mood; I do, after all, have a plan: I'll go to the shoot, make up some story about having been mugged or kidnapped, temporary amnesia perhaps, I'll add value at the shoot, redeem myself to the clients and the agency, thereby restoring Barry's confidence in my abilities, at which point I will make a deal with Barry that if I agree to work for nothing my salary will be divided up among Juliette and the others, something like that. One of the good things about LA, I've always thought, is it's easy to know which direction you are going; the sun rises in the east and sets in the west out here, no doubt about that, and there are hills to the east, there's an ocean to the west, and so on. It's simple. If you can see the beach and you go in the opposite direction you will hit the hills. If you can see the hills and go in the opposite direction you will hit the beach. And that's what I do. I see the hills and orient myself away from them, although there's not a through street coming off the medical center, so I have to cut across the UCLA campus. When I get to Sunset it isn't clear which direction goes toward the ocean, because Sunset is kind of curvy around here, and as I remember it hits the beach pretty far north of Santa Monica, and Shutters is at the southern end of Santa Monica anyway, so I take a right. I figure I'll get to some other major cross street and take that down toward the water. But as I'm trying to walk on Sunset, and cars are speeding past me on their way to the 405 and their jobs farther east or in the valley at one of the major studios, I realize that I can't really walk on Sunset, there's no sidewalk, at least in Westwood, and so I have to take the side streets.

I turn off Sunset at a street called Loring, beautiful homes from the 1940s, I am the only person walking on the sidewalks and I know this makes me a suspicious subject, and I turn onto Thayer and continue south. Then I turn right on Le Conte, counting the number of Mexicans cleaning their employers' driveways with air blowers, I'm up to four at this point, and several minutes later when I get on Westholme and then back to Le Conte, I take a left on Hills. After a few minutes I hit Loring again and realize that I've gone in a big circle. I'm not lost exactly, even though without my phone I have no idea where I am. I keep going till I get to Hilgard and I take that to West-wood. Westwood is a street I know, and it's wide. There's a bus that goes down it, there are no lawns or pneumatic Mexicans, so this route should be more direct. When I get to Pico I stop at the light, remembering that in LA you can actually get a ticket for jaywalking. I have no idea which direction I should be going but judging by where the sun is I turn left. I walk.

After half an hour I realize I should have hit the beach so obviously I'm going in the wrong direction; I'm heading east toward downtown LA. It's amazing what you miss when you're driving here. Every block features another two or three strip malls on either side of the road, and every strip mall is a kind of highly coded, veiled respository of people's hopes and dreams; every one is a Zolaesque Balzacian Dickens novel, a compen-dium, a vast collection of stories that on the surface look uncon-nected, random, but if you look deeper you'll see the threads that join them into a tapestry of human narrative and feeling. I'm standing at Pico and Sepulveda. There's a SuperCuts, SRS Shoes, Beds Etc., Good Feet, La Salsa Fresh Mexican Grill, and that's just on one corner. A little past it, LA Overhead Garage Doors. And just past that, Pet Supplies 4 You. I could stand here and make up a million tales about these places, the people who opened them, the customers who have come here for years, or I could just let my own memories flood into me; memories of my childhood, I'm looking at the Good Feet storefront, thinking about the time I stubbed my toe on the kitchen table running after my brother and I had to go see old Dr. Granach, some podiatrist we got referred to, because I had a blood blister. He gave me anaesthetic and then he popped it and drained the blood; afterward as I left I had no feeling in my right foot and it seemed like I was hobbling with one leg like a pirate ghost. And then my mother, she was still alive then, said I could stay home from school even though my father forbade such sissiness; she knew, as obviously this must have been one of her cogent periods, that I was easily shamed, and would have felt mortified limping around those hallowed halls. This is one of my best and most cherished memories of her.

A minute later I'm passing Pet Supplies 4 You, still floating in the past, remembering that we had a dog back then, and every Saturday when I went shopping with my dad one of our tasks was to buy a big bag of dog food, and we went to the discount pet store across the tracks, that's the kind of shopper my dad was, he was well-to-do but had been raised by parents who had lived through the Great Depression, so he was always looking for a deal. My mom, when she was with it enough to know what was happening or what day it was, would get angry because she said he could afford to buy dog food at the Kroger like everyone else, and get the better brand, and how does it make sense to drive all the way across town to the discount pet store for one bag of dog food, why don't you buy ten bags? My dad would just shrug, he didn't really have a reason why he did it that way, he just enjoyed it, and my mom would roll her eyes, how could anyone enjoy buying dog food? They didn't always get along. Our dog was named

Race, which is not a name you could give a dog today, I don't think, but my brother and I had not named him that for any sociological or politically concious reasons, we had named him after Race Bannon, who was a character on a 1960s cartoon called *Jonny Quest* that was in heavy rerun mode when we were kids in the '80s; they even tried briefly to revive the show with all new episodes in '86 for one season but it failed. In the cartoon, Jonny Quest and his father, Dr. Benton Quest, along with their bodyguard and pilot, Race Bannon (who had worked for a shadowy agency known as Intelligence One), travel in a jet plane to exotic locales in search of adventure. The other characters on the show were Hadji, an extraordinary Indian boy who had been adopted by Benton Quest, and Bandit, their bulldog. My brother and I had discussed at the time naming our dog Bandit, as you could imagine, with him staunchly in support of the idea and me opposed. I was eight years old but I remember making the argument that to name our dog Bandit was to merely steal someone else's dog name, the people who made the TV show *Jonny Quest*, it was theirs, their intellectual property, and thus entirely unoriginal if not wrong of us to copy them; we might as well name the dog Lassie. Tim persisted and so I suggested that we name him something else from within the *Jonny Quest* fanverse that would be both an homage to our love of the show during that golden time (as we were already beginning to age out of it) as well as a subtly ironic take on pop culture. I don't think I used the phrase "subtly ironic take on pop culture," I think I might have said it would be an "inside joke." My brother, whose name is Tim, as I said, and who today is an insurance broker in Dallas, and who is a year younger than I, would have nothing of it; he wanted to name our dog Bandit, even though he wasn't a bulldog, he was a Lab. But I continued in my insistence that it was ridiculous to name him Bandit, and everyone would think we were dolts, and that if he wanted to name him Bandit that I would from that day on have nothing to do with the animal. Parents were brought in and in the end I prevailed because I was the oldest; I believe that tears may have been involved. Whether you're right or wrong it's important to stand your ground and fight for what you believe in. But maybe I take these things too much to heart. Or is that simply what an Artist is? Someone who takes everything to heart? Am I an Artist? These days art is nothing but an alternative currency created for the purposes of money laundering. Walking east on Pico past blocks and blocks of Korean businesses, with signs in Korean and no English anywhere, I realize that if I had my phone with me I would call my brother and perhaps, if he failed to recognize my number and actually answered, I would apologize to him for being so insistent about naming our dog Race. That's exactly what I would do. After all, what would it have mattered in the final analysis if we had named him Bandit? The animal is no longer around. A few years after we got him, when we were ten and eleven, Race was hit by a car and killed instantly. That's what we were told. Much later, when I was in college and we had gone out and had a few beers together, my father told me the truth, which was that Race indeed had been hit by a car, yes, but he was not killed instantly at all, in fact he was writhing around in the middle of the street, and that Mr. Manning, our next-door neighbor in Canfield, had come out and yelled at my dad to do something about it, and my dad didn't know what to do. He had tried to pick up the dog but Race was so crazed that he bit my dad on the hand, and my father was freaking out about that, so the neighbor went into his garage and came back with a sledge hammer and he smashed our dog's skull with it, putting him out of his misery. Then the two men quickly put the dog in a bag and tossed him in the trash and hosed down the street before Tim and I got home from our tennis lessons. It was a Sunday. We were upset to hear that Race had died, Tim especially, me less so, as I remember it. But I've always had a sixth sense when it comes to lies, and I knew that something about my dad's story didn't add up. I don't know why, but I knew that Race had not been taken away by the police to be buried behind the police station, that didn't make sense to me, and so I looked in the trash and that's when I saw the bloody bag. I didn't open the bag but I knew there was a dead and mangled dog in it, I just knew. At first I didn't say anything to Tim about it but then I realized he should know, it might help him deal with his grief. That night I went into his room and told him that Race was in a plastic garbage bag in the trash can that would be emptied out Monday morning, if he didn't believe me he could go and look at it. Tim got up and we took a flashlight outside. It was late. I stepped back while Tim went up to the can and stood there, hesitating. He stood there for a minute debating, I guess, whether or not he really wanted to see his dead pet, and then turned back and looked at me.

"Should I open it?" he said, and I think it is the most serious question that anyone has ever asked me. "Should I open it?"

That's when I told him I was only kidding.

He stood and looked at me.

"I don't believe you," he said. "I think you're only saying that." He reached for the lid to pull it off and I came up behind him and put my hand on his hand to stop him. I pushed down hard and prevented him from doing it. We started fighting and I was bigger than him and I kept him from opening the lid. He started punching me with his fists, fury and grief a heady brew. Then our father came outside in his Brooks Brothers boxer shorts and shook his head. "What the hell is wrong with you kids?" he said to us, and then looked at Tim, who was crying at this point.

"Go to bed," he said.

When I went out drinking with my dad some twenty years later I told him what had transpired between me and Tim and Race that night. "You're dwelling on it," he said, and then got up and went to the bathroom. We got pretty drunk and ended up arguing about something (not my mom); we've never been in a bar together since.

By the time I get through the Korean section of Pico it's late afternoon, almost evening, I've been walking all day, which is good, I needed the exercise, I needed to sweat it out. I feel good. I'm almost downtown now; I see a taxi and wave it down and get in. A few minutes later we are on the 10 heading toward Santa Monica. It takes us nearly an hour because it's rush hour, but that's a lot faster than if I had walked back. I consider having the cabbie take me directly to the offices of Gangrape, the production company, but I can't remember where they are and besides, I need my laptop, my tablet, and my phone. When we get to Shutters on the Beach I pay the cabbie, the bellman opens the door for me, I go in, and as I'm heading across the lobby toward my room I see her standing there, twirling.

"Hey-dee-hi, heyo, yo!" she says with a broad smile that seems, insanely, genuine. It kind of lights up the place. "Fancy seeing you here!"

She's wearing American Apparel purple tights under a vintage Christian Dior skirt, on top of that she's got a frayed Van Halen T-shirt from the '80s and at the bottom of it all, ballet slippers, and on top, a purple sunset smudged below her eye. What is she doing? Is this some kind of art project? Of course she looks ridiculously beautiful (in the moment, it occurs to me that I have never been able to give her a tagline; I stand there, stunned, incapable of coming up with one, and AFTER MUCH COGITATION NOTHING SUITABLE COMES TO MIND™.)

"What are you doing here?" I ask, thinking that I am being disarming, or starting at a complete disadvantage, I don't know yet.

"Here? You mean LA?"

"Yeah I mean LA, I mean this hotel."

"I guess I'm doing the same thing you are."

"Me? And what am I doing?"

"Standing in the lobby of Shutters on the Beach."

"Oh is that what I'm doing? Thank you, I never would have guessed."

"Wow, really original sarcasm," she says with a wink. "Aren't you surprised to see me? Aren't you even going to thank me for the fruit basket?"

"Answer my question first," I say with a fake sternness.

"I'm here for the FreshIt shoot, dude!" she giggles. "Tom said I could come out as part of my internship. Don't worry, Eric, I paid my own way, I'm not screwing with your production budget, I know how important it is to put as much of every dollar on the screen as you can," she says, sounding like she's done some homework. "And I'm not stalking you, even ironically like before, I'm just trying to learn everything I can about the business. Love the 'boards, by the way, this is a great concept, I threw in some ideas for the director, hope you don't mind." It's the most she's said coherently since I met her.

"I think we need to talk," I say.

"About what? And where you been, yo, everyone thought you had quit and gone to Bali or something!"

"I've been walking," I say. "I've walked from one end of Los Angeles to the other and I can safely say it is the greatest city in the world."

"Cool," she says. Then we stand there for a moment and I go, "I have to get my phone. I have to get to the shoot."

She follows me back to my room; I don't object to this, as I might as well sit her down and have the talk that we need to have, explain to her all of the strange and difficult shit she has caused in my life including, tangentially, the recurrence of oddly pleasurable and at the same time vaguely troubling memories from my happy Midwestern childhood, including but not limited to my recent full-blown and highly entertaining sense of metanoia, an ancient Greek term meaning, "everything you know is wrong." We cross the pool deck and go down the hall, and when we get to my room my key card doesn't work; Intern says she thinks they may have checked me out because of the fact I disappeared for two-and-a-half days.

"Let's go to mine," she says.

We go to her room, it's one level up and around the corner on the ocean side. I know technically speaking it's not a good idea for me to go with her to her room, but the new addition to my medication regimen that they gave me at UCLA had taken away most all my sexual proclivity, although my penis is, I think, sort of semitumescent as always. We get to her room and I ask her how she's affording this room if the company isn't paying for it and she isn't getting remunerated as an intern. This is my proof, I realize, this is my proof that she is under the employ of Barry, brought in here to mess with me, to destroy me so they can get out of my contract.

"My parents," she says. "I told them an internship is like graduate school. It's expensive but it's the only way to get a job anymore, and so they sprung for it."

"There are cheaper hotels than Shutters on the Beach," I remind her. "I think the Four Seasons is cheaper than this place."

"I hate the Four Seasons," she says as she opens her door, and I imagine her having an affair with Barry Spinotti at the Four Seasons; he's been flying out here to do what he called some "triage" in our LA office recently: got it, Bar, say no more. We walk in. She lets the door slam closed and we stand there in the dark. The room, what I can see of it, is bigger than mine. She looks at me and this makes me uncomfortable so I go to the curtains and throw them open; she has a view of the bay. Then I go to the bathroom and turn on all the lights.

"Harrison Ford stays at this hotel when he's in LA," she says.

"I know."

She tosses her Freitag messenger bag on the bed and looks at me again. Then she sits down.

"What are you doing?" I ask her.

"I don't know what you're talking about," she says. She reaches for the phone. "I'm going to call the front desk and see what happened to your room. What was the number again?"

"Put the phone down," I say in my serious voice.

She puts the phone down. "What?"

"We need to talk."

"About what?"

"About that eye."

"What about it?" she says. "Is it a problem or something?"

"Well when a nineteen-year-old girl tells her employer that one of her superiors fucked her and punched her in the face, yeah, that does cause some problems."

There's a long pause and then she says, "What are you talking about?"

"I was told you told them at Tate that I punched you in the face."

"You were?"

"Yes."

Then she laughs.

"Why would I tell them that? Are you fucking with me? I fell into the doorjamb in your loftlike aparment, as you call it, remember, the night we did those Black Beauties I bought from that French guy at Dressler. Shit, I wish we hadn't done that. What were we thinking?" She smiles in a jaunty way. "It was fun, though. And who told you I'm nineteen? I'm twenty-four. Look, I get that you can't have a relationship with me now that we work in the same company, do you think I want to get us in trouble or something? No way. I'm trying to figure out my life, not fuck it up. By the way did you watch that Alejandro Jodorowsky movie I left on your desk? *El Topo*? I really think you would love it."

I'm facing the big picture windows and she's sitting on the bed, facing me, so she's mostly in shadow. I'm having a hard time reading her, so I step back and turn on some lights. There are about sixteen light switches by the door and I just slide them all up so now the place is lit up like a sound stage. Every one of the five hundred threads in each of the sheets is hot white and every nook and crevice of every decorative conch shell is glowing pink and florid as it would in, say, Florida.

"Listen," I say, "I don't know what kind of game you think you're playing with me, but it isn't funny."

"No?" she says, allowing the tiniest bit of pouty girlishness into her voice. "Why don't you think it's funny?" I'm standing right over her now and she takes her eyes off my eyes and looks at my belt. Then she's reaching to undo it but I step away.

"Don't do that," I say.

"Why?" she says. "Why not? Oh come on, no one will know, and I promise we won't do it again, you can totally trust me on this."

I consider telling her the whole story, giving her the entire rundown that a) I'm not in the mood because I checked myself into the hospital because I was having a panic attack and thought I was going to die, and then I trashed the ER and they put me in the psych ward, where they gave me Halcion and Abilify and zinfandel and who knows what other antidepressants and antipsychotics, which have limited my desire to have sex and b), I don't even remember what b) is, I'm trembling so much as she undoes me.

"Because I don't want to," I say.

"No? You don't want to what? Do you realize we haven't even properly made love yet? Yeah, we've done shit, but we haven't actually had intercourse and I think it would be something of a shame if we didn't know what that felt like." Her little pouty voice again. I stand there shaking a bit, inside, maybe it's just my stomach, due to the fact I forgot to eat during the long Pico journey. There were so many options and I had decided I would investigate them all visually, at least the taco-related ones, and stop at what seemed like the best on my way back to the beach, but that didn't happen. She gets up and takes a step toward me and smiles, tilts her head to one side, this really is her best feature, not her face exactly but the youth and I suppose guilelessness that emanate from it when she smiles. She is too beautiful right now to attempt description; I don't move, I don't speak.

"I want to take a picture of you looking just like that," she says.

"Why?" I say.

"Because there's this website, it's called Look At This Fucking Douchebag, I could put your photo on it!" Then she laughs. "Just kidding. You look nice. You look different out here, you look rested, it does you good."

"Funny," I say. Then she tells me about a series of pix that she and her friend took back in New York, they found these little stuffed animals that someone had thrown away, and they also found a Cincinnati Bengals jacket, and they put the stuffed animals inside the Bengals jacket in various funny and compromising positions and took dozens of pictures with their phones and made a Tumblr of it and got something like twenty thousand views in the first week.

"Cool," I say, not really understanding anything at this point.

"It was Kaytlin's idea," she goes on. "She's an artist."

"I don't know if I can believe a word of what you're telling me," I say.

"Good," she says. "I like it that way."

Then she gives me that look again and takes another step toward me; I don't back off, I just stare at her. She takes my belt and undoes it. Then I grab hold of her wrists and stop her before she can unzip the AGs.

"Don't."

"Aw," she says, maybe giving up for now. "And I was going to give you a Deep Whatsis." I don't know what that is; I just look at her blankly.

"What's a Deep Whatsis?" I ask.

"Exactly. This boyfriend of mine, he said it was beyond the power of the human mind to comprehend, so that's what he dubbed it," she says. "But I made it up. It's a super deluxe blowjob is all, using this certain kind of oil and, um . . . some other things."

She looks up at me and smiles. I don't smile back. Though I want to. But I know what will happen if I do.

"Oh well," she says, "oh well."

I look down at her, wishing I was still in the hospital, at least there I was safe. Ten seconds later I'm lying on the bed, she's pulling my pants off and tossing them onto the floor. She reaches into her messenger bag and takes out a bottle of almond oil and a box of Fisherman's Friend cough drops. I prop up my head on about five goose-down pillows and watch as she takes the top off the almond oil bottle, very slowly, and pours some on my now fully erect dick. She rubs it in with her left hand. Then she pops two lozenges into her mouth and upturns the bottle. She empties it and swishes the oil around between her cheeks, sucking for a minute on the menthol drops. Then she straddles me and gives me a look before going down on me, thrusting my cock into her fully lubricated gob, and thus it begins. The almond oil, she explains later, is an excellent a lubricant, and the menthol acts as a stimulant, increasing sensation in the nerve endings, and indeed it's the first time I've ever experienced anything remotely like this. Her tongue and mouth go up and down and around my member with supreme conviction. She's adept at understanding when I'm about to explode and backs off long enough to keep me in the game, over and over, again and again. This goes on, as I remember, pretty much the rest of the afternoon and into the night; when finally she lets me get off I see stars behind my eyes.

When I wake up it's dark and she's in bed with me and we're naked. My face is up against her shoulder and my arm is wrapped around her. She senses me moving and shifts toward me.

"Hey, sleepyhead," she says, kissing me lightly on my nose. "You were so sweet."

Was I? With one eye open I look at her and try to focus. I want to move my arm, I don't know how it got where it is, under her, my fingers entwined in hers on the other side of her body.

"I thought we said this wasn't going to happen," I say.

"I know, I didn't think we would actually have sex like actual sex-havers either," she says. "But oh well, we did, didn't we, and we survived."

"We had sex?" I asked, possibly the dumbest question ever.

"Yes, dummy," she says, "we made love. After the, you know."

Then she kisses me on the nose again and jumps up out of bed, her hair dancing on her head and off her shoulders like pre-CG glitter falling from the Good Witch's wand.

"Let's go to the beach!"

I look over at the so-called digital clock by the bed. It reads 4:49 AM.

"Let's go swimming at the beach and then we'll get breakfast!" This seems like a terrible idea to me but I am wide awake now, and my head is clear for the first time in at least two years if not my life, and my penis is soft. Hallelujah. It's not yet 8 AM in New York, way too early to call Barry and explain to him my Plan Moving Forward, and so after a bit of coaxing I get dressed and we sneak out. We go out via the pool deck and down some steps to the bike path, each of us carrying a massive white towel from the hotel. There's nobody here, no joggers or bikers, and even the early morning cleanup crews haven't arrived. We trudge across the black beach toward the black water, heading slightly south toward Venice to avoid some kind of maintenance dig going on opposite the hotel; the sky is ink past the ocean but behind us there's enough of a glow to indicate that day will in fact dawn on us in due time.

When we get to the water she drops her towel on the sand and takes off the CD skirt and the Van Halen tee. In the dim ochre wash cast by the sodium-vapor lights above the bike path, she looks like a wisp of cotton candy held aloft by an anime princess.

Naked, she rushes out and disappears headlong into the waves.

As she moves into the surf I take my time pulling my pants and shirt off; up on the path I see a lone runner jogging toward the Palisades, a woman in a blue-and-white sweatsuit, with a visor on her head and an iPhone in her hand, its twin cords making a V around her chin. She sees us skinnydipping kids and looks over and seems to smile. I give her a feeble wave-like wave in return and she continues on without breaking her stride. I turn back to watch Intern frolicking in the sea, and feeling suddenly very bare I head into the water and it's frigid. My arms are wrapped around my chest and I am mock shivering to cover my actual shivering as the water reaches my knees, splashing my balls and shrinking them to the size of dried peas. Far out in the distance I can see a couple of lights, perhaps they are sailboats that have moored overnight, more likely they are tankers or oceangoing barges on their way to the docks at San Pedro. Behind me I can barely make out the edge of the cliffs that rise up to Main Street, where Sushi Roku is, and I imagine a small army of illegals there already, mopping up and heaving rotting fish parts into a dumpster in the back. Intern turns and sees me heading toward her and laughs.

"Come on, you! It's not that cold!"

I do a kind of fake shiver again and jump up as a wave comes toward me, turning around so that it hits me in the ass. Then I move quickly out, pulled in part by the backwash, and when the next wave comes I go for it, dropping down and to my side and just letting it slam into me. Now I'm completely wet and freezing.

"That's more like it!" she says. She comes up to me and puts her arms around me and with the next wave we are floating together in the water and being pushed back toward shore.

"Let's go farther out!" she says.

"This is fine," I say.

Then she kisses me, and holds me, sort of as if we are lovers now, as if our night together in the same bed, her arm over my side from time to time, my arm on top of her, has changed things between us. Maybe it has. She looks up at me and smiles and I relax a bit. Perhaps I've been overreacting to her advances, I think, perhaps this is nothing more than a frisky party girl who likes to get fucked up and have sex with guys who don't even know her name because she's young and none of it matters, none of it de-perfumes the soul for more than an hour, or a night. Perhaps that's all this is, here's a girl who likes making guys happy, likes the few moments of feigned intimacy that it provides, likes hanging out at Glasslands and Death By Audio and maybe giving head to some cool guy from the band she just saw, in the john just before closing time; it's not a totally wasted night even if he doesn't call you, which he won't, although he might send a booty text at some point in the coming week or two. Perhaps she's got these awful rich asshole parents, the angry alcoholic type-A Wall Street dad and the OxyContin-addled Botoxified mom with the bogus not-for-profit foundation that gives laptops to endangered birds. She grew up on the Upper East Side enduring her parents' horrible, asinine friends, she had to put up with the idiocies of one of those tony Daltony schools, and in silent revenge against them she became loose, she became lost, revenge is sweet and bitter, Mommy, look at me now—but no, stop, stop for once, that's not it. She's not what thinking made her, not at all. She's a girl, she's here, she's lovely.

"This is kind of embarrassing," I say, "but I'm not really even sure what your name is."

"No way!"

"Suri or Sari or something but I don't remember. I'm really sorry about that. I feel like a jerk."

"It's Sabi!" she says. "Short for Sabine. My mom was very like hippie slash Euro, she was into German movies and shit. I think there was like this character in this Fassbinder film, I can't remember which one, I've blocked it out. I saw it once and I was literally like 'Oh My God this is not his best work why did you name me after her!' "

I peer down at her face and for a moment I feel something, something akin I suppose to what happiness feels like, or maybe it's only compassion or tenderness, they're all interrelated in some way. Is it an emotional-slash-psychological question or are we merely talking etymology, and then I stop thinking and I kiss her. I stop kissing her and look at her—I may be smiling at this point?—and kiss her again. We kiss in the waves for a bit and then we stop.

"Sabi," I go. "I think I, um, I think I'm . . ."

And then I say it.

"In love with you."

She freezes for a moment and then looks at me and then looks away. Did I just ruin everything? That was not my intent.

"I'm sorry, did I . . . ? Should I have not . . . ?"

"No, no," she says, "it's cool."

"Is something wrong?"

"No, no, it's cool," she says again. "I think I kind of, um, you know, like, with you, too."

And now I look at her, as if for the first time, but she is not looking at me, she's looking out to the ocean, as if she sees something happening there on the dark horizon, the apocalypse forming, warships approaching, and so I look out there too, into the darkness, but there's nothing, even the tankers and their tiny lights have left the scene. What are we looking at? What are we looking for? And when I turn and look back at her she isn't there, she's running—no, running up to the shore, kicking up her knees, bounding over waves, and sprinting up onto the sand.

"Sabi! Hey!" I cry out. "Wait, stop, what are you doing?"

"Leave me alone!" she seems to shout back at me and then I start running after her, she's scooping up the hotel towel and her clothes in it and she's running south toward Venice, running as fast as she can. By the time I emerge from the waves to give chase, she's pretty far ahead of me, I run as hard as I can on the sand but I'm not really gaining much ground on her. Coming up the path I see the jogger standing there, the woman with the blue-and-white sweatsuit and the visor, she's holding her iPhone up at me like she's just Instagrammed a weird shot of a naked man chasing a naked girl on the beach. Then she starts jogging again, back up toward the PCH, and I have no choice but to watch Sabi disappear, thinking, pondering, why did I say what I said to her? Could I have worded it differently? If I had dropped the "um, I think" before the "I love you" would that have made a difference? If I had said it in another way, "I have strong feelings for you" perhaps, or "you know, I really like you a lot," would that have garnered a different result?

When I get back to the beach outside Shutters my clothes are gone and the sun is coming up. I see a trash truck emptying trash bins and realize they must have tossed my Adriano Goldschmieds and Hugo shirt; perhaps I can persuade our finance department to reimburse me if I can find the original receipts. I look around for something to hide behind, a newspaper, a plastic bag, but the beach has been swept clean. I hike up naked to the hotel and just walk into the lobby and up to the desk and for some reason speak in a half-British accent.

"Pardon me but someone has just nicked my jeans," I say. "Might I trouble you for a key?"

Wearing a robe they provided at the desk, I cross the empty pool deck and go down the hallway to my room; I gather my things, put them into my suitcase, pack away my laptop, and consider taking lots of pharmaceuticals but decide against it. I throw on some pants and a shirt and my J. Lindeberg suit jacket and grab my phone off the desk, and just as I am about to put it in one of the pockets I decide to look at it; there are a few messages but no e-mails from work, possibly the server is down? I stare at the phone's clock feature and watch the minute change a few times; it does so about every sixty seconds. I text and call Tom Bridge and leave him a message inquiring as to the whereabouts of the shoot. I call my assistant back in New York and she doesn't pick up either. I try her cell and her home phone, nothing, weird. Then I find Sabi's text, the one I didn't delete, and I hit "reply" and the 347 number appears.

I hesitate and then I call; her phone rings, she doesn't answer, which I suspected would happen, the voice mail tells me that her voice mailbox is full. I go back to the front desk and ask for a cab. One comes almost immediately. I give the cabdriver the address of the Gangrape offices, which I got from the little card on the fruit basket that finally did arrive. The card had said "Eric, Here's to a hoppin' fine time in LA! Lots of love, Your friends at Gangrape."

As we head down Ocean Boulevard into Venice I listen to the messages; one is from Tom Bridge wondering why I'm not meeting them for dinner, one is from Seth Krallman wondering if I still want to pick up his car or not, one is from Lynette my headhunter singsong asking how things are going and wondering if I have any interest in an ECD job at Grey, and one is from Barry, who is not wondering anything at all, I doubt he's ever experienced wonder in his life. But that's the one I pay attention to: "Eric, this is Barry. Please call me at your earliest convenience."

The Gangrape offices are housed in an old warehouse on the railroad tracks in Culver City. When I get there I pay the driver and go inside. It's a big open space with a skylight and a plywood halfpipe in the center; the Gangrape directors are all known for their amazing skate videos. The Gangrape director that we hired, Brian Sisto, is twenty-seven and goes by the moniker Psyk, as in "sick" or "ill." Brian's bio claims that he was homeless for a time, living with the skate kids on Venice Beach, which is when he began documenting the skater thing, and photography and video saved his life, but I happen to know that his father is Vito Sisto, the reputed mobster-turned-producer, head of production at a porn studio in the '90s.

Just inside the Gangrape headquarters, sitting at a big long desk made of traffic pylons are two scorching-hot girls, one blonde and one redhead. I approach the blonde and tell her I'm with Tate, I'm the creative director, I just got into town and need to know where the shoot is, I lost my call sheet. She seems confused for a moment and runs back to talk to someone and then returns.

"Here's a copy," she says as she hands the call sheet to me. "It has the address of the location, it's a house in Mar Vista not far from here, those are the GPS coordinates."

"You think I could walk there?" I ask her.

"Um." She pauses and thinks. Then she turns to the redhead. "Can you walk to Mar Vista from here?"

"What's Mar Vista?" Ginger asks.

"It's this little neighborhood with these like really cool midcentury modern houses?"

"Where is it?"

"I think it's like just past Cloverfield?"

"Cloverfield? I thought that was a movie?"

"It's a street?"

"It is?"

"I think so?"

At this point I'm walking out. It takes me a few minutes to walk to Venice Boulevard and find a cab but I do; the cabdriver has no idea where Mar Vista is, he doesn't know where Cloverfield is, but he does have GPS and so we punch the numbers in and he takes me there. It's nowhere near Cloverfield. At one point the GPS gets the direction of a one-way street wrong and we have to go around the block but this is a minor inconvenience; I don't mind taking more time than needed because I'm looking in every direction, hoping to see a naked girl carrying a Shutters towel.

When I get to the location the shoot is in full swing. I can hear classic hip-hop (50 Cent's "Gunz Come Out") coming from inside the house, which is a modest early '60s job with a slab for parking and a jaunty roof, the kind of house you'd buy back then if you couldn't afford a real house, and now they go for two-point-five. I pass some crew guys carrying a couch out the door, stepping over cables, another guy carrying C-stands to the cube truck, and when I get to set I see an actress, midthirties, brown straight hair, bangs, attractive without being pretty—or is it pretty without being hot—and instantly I know that this is our Abby. If I had been involved in the casting she might not have been so perky, so ingratiatingly "mom-ish" but what difference does it make now? As the camera rolls Abby is gyrating ridiculously to the Fiddy track, with her head high in the air, and I suss out immediately that this is Psyk's take on the commercial, that instead of the quick little sniff and a smile that the creatives had spent the past six months discussing endlessly with the clients (is it a smile of Enjoyment? is it a smile of Satisfaction? is it a smile of Homemaker Pride?) he's decided that Abby is to *celebrate* the lovely new scent provided by FreshIt World of Scents. It's genius. The scent is like her orgasm, the orgasm she has never experienced with her unemployed husband, or with the neighbor she fucks occasionally in his car, only not anymore, she feels too guilty about it, and she would never buy a vibrator, what if Eddy found it? etc. And so FreshIt World of Scents becomes therefore so much more than the sign of being a good mom, it's something she does for herself, in private, the scent transports her to a virtual world of her own making, a world nobody knows about, her own velvety world of self-gratification.

FWS IS A GIFT YOU GIVE YOURSELF!

I look around the room, at every member of the crew, the agency producers, the creatives, the clients from Unabrand, the homeowners who are making fifteen grand renting their house out for the day. None of them are her.

Where the fuck did she go?

The music stops and some chubby hairy white guy in an Asics running suit and a flat-billed MOBBING hat on sideways jumps up and starts clapping and screaming at the top of his lungs. This is Pysk himself and he's super happy with the take. Abby, for her part, looks exhausted and humiliated; you can always tell the real actresses, they're the ones who smile constantly during the process because if they ever stopped they'd fly into a rage, the hacks are the ones actually enjoying themselves. I head over to video village where the creatives and Tom Bridge are sitting in director's chairs.

"Hey, guys," I say. Tom looks at me and then back at the monitors.

"You made it," he says. I tell him I had to work from the hotel on something, a crisis on the Allstate account, sorry I haven't been in touch. He doesn't seem to care, and then one of the PAs jumps up and offers me a chair. I say, no, no, thanks, I'll stand.

The rest of the shoot goes as planned, although I can't really concentrate on what's happening. I do my share of fake bonding with the clients, two guys in identical khaki pants and blue shirts and Bluetooth headsets, and I send a couple of texts to Sabi, no reply, and a couple of times I feel phantom vibrations in my pocket, pulling out my phone to realize there's nothing there. I feel compelled, as long as I'm here, to make a show of adding value and so I offer up the suggestion that when Abby's husband comes home, in the shot where we see him notice the fresh new scent, he should take his hands and actually widen out his nostrils to get a better hit of fragrant air. Elbows akimbo, how funny! This is of course the stupidest idea that I could have conjured up, and I know it, but as creative director I also know that everyone will agree with me, wholeheartedly, despite thinking how dumb I am. Even Psyk, the radical rebel white gangsta skatepunk rocker agrees with me, he says SUH-WEET! like five times, and that's how I know he is a tool; no doubt in a couple of years he will be a major feature guy. Sitting there watching Abby's "husband" Eddy on the monitor as he tries to widen his nostrils out like a jackass, I have to remind myself I'm only doing this so that Barry can't claim I'm not doing my job; when I get back to New York I'll need him on my team to make everything right.

That night we all go out to dinner at Koi. After the eda-mame steamed in Finnish lake ice slow-melted over smoking Brazilian rosewood, I step out and call Sabi's number again but I still can't leave a message. Psyk doesn't drink so Tom and I order the double flight of sake for ourselves and then an hour later another one. By the time we leave, around ten, we are staggering. We get the line producer to take us to Chez Jay's near the hotel. By 2 AM it's just Tom and I at the bar and I ask him if he knew where Intern was.

"She was at pre-pro," he said. "But I didn't see her today."

"Maybe she got sick of advertising and went back to New York," I say.

"The whole dancing-slash-inner-joy thing was her idea."

"You mean that Fiddy Cent shit?"

"Well, we won't use that track in the spot, we'll create something more amenable to the target demo, but yeah. The dancing. The inner joy. Psyk will take credit for it but it was her idea."

Tom gives me a look and I can't tell if he knows more than he's saying or if he's just so shitfaced that his expression is mutant.

"Are you serious?" I say.

"Maybe," he says and looks away.

"No, really," I say. "How did that work? You let an intern ideate at the pre-pro?"

"I guess so."

"Is she good? What do you know about her?"

"Less than you," he says.

"What the fuck is that supposed to mean?"

"Look, Eric, I don't know anything about the slut," he says. "OK?"

"Don't call her a slut, it's not nice."

"Copy that," he says and I stare at him, try to get what he's getting at, if anything, and then he laughs and sticks his fist toward me and holds it there for a while and so we fist bump. I stare at him some more; something's eating at the guy and no matter how long I sit here looking at him I'm not able to divine what it might be. Down the bar there's a sexy burnt-out woman who's been looking up from her phone at us from time to time, Tom had bought her a drink about an hour ago but she barely acknowledged it. Now as he gets up and slurs his way toward the bathroom she turns to him and smiles. He stops and tries to say something funny to her about her shoes and I realize this is my window and I leave. It's a short walk to Shutters and I get there without incident. Back at the hotel I notice there's a new guy working the desk. I ask him if he's seen the girl who's got one of the beach-facing rooms that they said weren't available but clearly were.

"Suite three twelve," I say.

He looks at his screen and then back at me. "The occupant of that room checked out earlier."

"Are you sure?" I ask.

"Yes, I'm sure," he says.

"Do you know where she went? Sabine? We work together and I . . . um . . . I'm her boss."

"I don't know," he says.

"One other thing: her bill? Can you tell me if she paid with her own card or was she charged as a part of our production? Or on another card?"

"I wouldn't have that information," he says.

"Thank you," I say, not pressing him. Then I go to my room. I open the blinds and look out the window at the parking lot. I crank the window open a few inches so I can hear the sound of the surf and a guy has some rap-inflected R&B, possibly Frank Ocean, coming from his car down below, which is weird given my view. I then close the window and sit on my bed. We never should have gone swimming. We should have just gone back to sleep and then gotten up late and ordered room-service omelets, with the sprig of rosemary on the plate, and the orange slice, twisted into a mobius-shaped bowtie symbolizing forever, symbolizing us, and if we had done that, if we had stayed in and ordered the omelets, everything would be fine. I think again of calling her to, what, to say what? I love you? I don't even know if I do. To apologize? For what? Would she even listen? Instead I just compose a note, a long SMS, and stare at it, and recompose it, a few times, making it longer and then shorter, much shorter, adding and subtracting the requisite layers of irony, finally landing on utter neutrality, utter pictographic simplicity tinged with a subtext of bemusement if not helplessness, and after several minutes of consternation I finally hit send:

?

The next morning I check out early and take a taxi to LAX. There won't be a seat in first back to New York for a few hours and so I wait in the private lounge till I can get one. I figure I might as well get it over with so I call Barry back in the office. His secretary puts him through.

"Barry, are you firing me?" I ask him outright.

"Why the fuck would I do that? Are you out of your mind?" he says.

"I'm just getting a vibe," I say, "that's all. And if you are, I want you to know, it's exactly what I would do to me if I were you."

"You're nuts," he says. "When you coming back?" I tell him I'm on the next flight but it won't get me into JFK until after six so he'll be way up the Saw Mill by that time. Then I tell him how great these spots are going to turn out, how the director really juiced the concept, trying to make it sound like I'm doing my job. He doesn't seem to care.

"And I got to ask you about Dr. Look," I say. "Apparently he doesn't exist."

"Come see me first thing tomorrow," is all he says and then hangs up.

I work on the screenplay while I wait in the lounge. The beginning is completely wrong and so I start to write it again. But the flight boards a little early and, although we leave the gate a few minutes late due to some issue with the onboard video system, they manage to make up the time heading east and we land at JFK on time. I have about one tenth of a glass of the worst pinot grigio I have ever tasted in my life and the ricotta-filled pasta shells are equally revolting, but the ice cream is OK. At the baggage claim a heavyset Syrian man named Aki is waiting for me with my name written twice in dry-erase marker on a white plastic board: NYE, Nye. The Syrian drives me home listening to Fox News the whole way, and when I get home, for a millisecond I think that I'm in the wrong apartment.

The next morning I go to the office, that air-conditioned slaughterhouse of the soul, as it has been called, around 8 AM, at least an hour and a half earlier than usual. I go into my space and close the door. No phone calls or e-mail. On a notepad I write down the names of the people I have fired over the last two years so I can try to rectify the nightmare, or at least apologize to them in some way; can you do that on Facebook? It comes to forty-two. For a second I consider setting up a Kickstarter to raise money to give back to the ones I wronged, this would probably get covered by the *Times* and thereby help my screenwriting presence. Then I call HR at her desk and on her cell and she doesn't respond. I look out my office and see that my assistant isn't in yet; this is odd, she drops her kid off and is here by 8:30 most mornings, long before I am. Then I stare out the window at a guy on Tenth Avenue setting up his kebab cart. At around ten I call Barry's line and tell his person, Agnes, that I want to see him ASAP. She says she was about to call me because, what a coincidence, Barry wants to set up a meeting with me, at 10:30, am I available? Hmm, um, let me look, yes, I say, and she hangs up. I fold and pocket the list of names I wrote up, to show Barry what I've been going through, and then I kill some time on the internet and go to the bathroom; now that my permanent chub has somewhat subsided I can pee at a urinal again, yay. Then I go to the elevators and mumble good morning to one of the creatives from the pharma department whose name I never bothered to learn, and then I say I'm really sorry I have jet lag, what's your name again? "And how's everything with you?" he asks politely. "This place is fucked," I say. "Seriously. If anything comes along that looks halfway decent, take it." Then I ride up to Barry's floor and walk toward his office, left down the middle hallway and left again toward the corner. When I get there I know immediately how this is going to go because I see HR Lady stepping into Barry's lair and closing the door;

she didn't see me arrive so for the next I'm guessing twenty seconds I have the upper hand.

Agnes looks up at me and grimaces, says that Barry just took a call from Manchester and he should be ready for me in half a minute. I lean back against a credenza and consider my options. I don't like waiting for Barry and there's really no reason I have to go through with this, to have him pull out the photo of me and Sabi naked on the beach, the one the jogger took, and tell me my behavior is unfit for someone of my station, or this venerable firm. I turn to Agnes.

"Give Barry a message for me," I say. "Tell him to go fuck himself." And then I turn around and head toward the elevators. When I get there, one of them opens, and off step Damon and Terry, and they head toward Barry's office; that's when I realize I'm doing this all wrong. I need to let it happen, just as it happened to the rest of them. So I head back, Agnes sees me as Damon and Terry get there, and Barry's door opens. HR is standing there, and I go toward her.

"Hi Eric," she says. "How are you?"

"I'm good," I say, and go inside. Barry is sitting behind his desk, I take my seat on his couch and notice that the Smoke Eater is off.

"What's up?" I say. "How's everybody this morning?"

There's an uncomfortable pause and then Barry coughs and says, "We're good, Eric, how are you?"

"I'm here," I say. "So let's do it." I turn to HR Lady, Helen, and look at her one last time. Her eyes are not glistening. But she seems sadder than I've ever seen her before.

"I'm very sorry to say this, Eric," she says, "but we're going to have to let you go."

Three minutes later I am heading down Tenth Avenue toward my Chase branch, a free man. I take out my phone thinking that I will be able to enjoy it for probably another minute or two before they shut it down. I call Seth and tell him I will meet him at Balthazar for breakfast and that he should drive there and park in a decent lot. "Don't worry, I'll pay for the parking," I tell him. He's pissed that I woke him up; in truth he should be pissed about a lot of things, including the shitty way that I treat him in general, all the time, but chiefly he should be pissed at his father for fucking up the family financials so badly, raising Dr. Namaste in a cloud of abject privilege and then day-trading the entire fortune away in less than a year. I go to my bank and then an hour later Seth and I are having café au lait and Bellinis and eggs Benedict together and I am handing the unfortunate shithead an envelope filled with twenty-five one-thousand-dollar bills.

"Twenty-five?" he says. I tell him I just quit my job, it's the best I can do. He thinks about it. I know what's going through his head, that since I quit I'm little or no use in terms of getting him into the advertising business, for the time being at least, so why should he let me screw him on the price of a used Range Rover? On the other hand, this was twenty-five large that he would not have to tell his parents about for quite a while, twenty-five grand worth of artisanal bespoke curated locally

sourced cage-free goat cheeses delivered to his shithole apartment, twenty-five grand that would forestall the inevitable real-
ization that he had ruined his life, or his parents had ruined his
life, and there was nothing he could do about it now but enjoy
the ride. He sighs and looks away and then he tosses his café au
lait down a little too hard and the sound makes the girl at the
next table turn around and look at us.

"No fucking way," Seth says to me. "We agreed to thirty."

"Oh come on, man," I say to him, "do your brother a solid.
I need a vehicle, dude. I need some freedom. I was just sacked."

"I thought you said you quit?"

"They were about to sack me so I quit in protest," I answer.

"In protest to what? Your own assholiness?" he says. It's
a pretty funny line but I don't laugh. "And why do you need a
vehicle if you don't even have a job?" I tell him that not having a
job means I can drive around and see shit and he can come with
me, we'll go to Niagara Falls or something.

"You're such a fucking liar, Eric, you know that?" he
says. "You would never go to Niagara Falls and if you did you
wouldn't bring me, you'd bring some twenty-two-year-old
barista or something." Here he goes, I now know this is going to
be his gusher; what took him so long? "In fact you're a fucking
pathological liar," he says. "You need help. You talk this whole
radical Occupy the Man line of bullshit but really you're the
fucking enemy, Jack, you're the one perpetuating the whole sys-
temic materialist ideology you pretend to despise."

"Duh," I say. "And that's why I quit. And furthermore,"
I go on, "I know everything you're about to say about me now,

because you bore me off my ass, Seth, you make me want to blow you I'm so bored." Then I laugh and mock punch him in the shoulder; I'm starting to like him for once. But Seth will not be quieted. He goes on for another five minutes about all the ways in which I am a shit human being with me agreeing wholeheartedly with him and then suddenly he stops and begins to tear up—to cry, right there at Balthazar during the late-breakfast rush. He's shuddering with big spasms of anger and humiliation and I suppose regret because nothing, nothing that I say, not even when I put a hand on his trembling arm as a sign of emotional support, can quell the sobs. Deep, deep from the bottom of his soul the man-boy Seth spews out his slobbering gasps. I toss a hundy on the table and grab him by the arm. "Come on you fucking idiot," I say to him and pull him out onto the street.

Once we're standing on Spring I grab him by the shoulders and mock shake him. "Snap out of it, man," I say, "wake up." He says he doesn't even know what he's doing, he's been seriously depressed for weeks, his life is so meaningless, ever since his girlfriend left him, etc., etc.

"But I thought you left *her*?" I say.

"Technically I did," he blubbers. "Technically in the sense that I was the one who said the words 'I'm breaking up with you' but that was because I thought she was about to leave me for this other guy and I couldn't bear it, only it turned out she wasn't even into him but by the time I found out it was too late. I'm a coward and I'm a loser and I have no courage, and without her I'm nothing, the only thing I had was my car and the hope you would get me a job and now I don't even have my car and you just got fired. Fuck!"

"Come on," I say, "let's get a drink."

We walk a block down the street and go into the Shark Bar. There are always people here, even at 11 AM so we don't feel too pathetic. We sit at the bar. I look around and am reminded of the story of the arrest of the notorious serial killer Ted Bundy, when they confronted him with the horror of his crimes, his response was to be surprised that anyone would care. "There are so many people!" he said. "Look!"

Seth and I start with beer, figuring we'll have a couple of late-morning pints, no harm in that, and then go sleep it off, but the beers lead to the whiskies, and we just keep going. By five o'clock in the afternoon Seth has told me everything about his sad life and he is begging me to pay twenty thousand dollars for the car, refuses to accept more because he feels guilty for saying all those terrible things about me.

"What right do I have to criticize you, of all people, you're a functional human being," he says, "you're at the top of your game!" Then he confesses that he wrote my Wikipedia bio based on stuff I had drunkenly told him over the years. I laugh and say the whole thing was no big deal, in fact it was pretty funny, and if I still had a job I would hire him on the spot. Then we cook up a plan for him to hack the Wiki entries for all the top creative directors in New York; he'll make a video of it with his phone and post it to AdRanter and the job offers will come flying in.

Then he starts in again on the depression thing, that maybe he should check himself into a hospital, it's really bad, he doesn't know what to do, and he's massaging the envelope in his jacket pocket that has his money minus the $5K I lightened from it, which I will now need to pay my rent.

"Don't go to the hospital," I tell him. "They don't know how to help anyone." I then tell him about my two-dot-five days at UCLA but he's not paying attention. I tell him about the times my mother was in and out for her various mental conditions and look where it got her. He's thinking faraway thoughts.

"You know how much brown I could score with this right now?" he says, fingering the envelope. Brown is his word for heroin, even though real brown hasn't been available in New York for a decade now, I read that in *Fader* once.

"No, how much?" I ask him as if I care. He tells me he knows where he could get enough of the stuff that, once he cuts it with a basic store-bought laxative, he could sell it on the street for ten times as much.

"That's nearly a quarter mil," he says. "That makes a pretty sizable down payment on a sweet place in the 'wick, set myself up, do my art, all kinds of shit, dog," he says.

"Dog!" I say in solidarity. "You're drunk."

"Dog!" he says again in a louder voice. "So what? It's a killer idea."

He's really getting worked up about this business plan of his. I'm guessing that he hit bottom these past few hours and will be from now on moving back into a manic phase. I've seen this pattern with him several times before. He's way more fun when manic, if you catch him at the right time, but it doesn't last long, so you have to just go with it.

"I don't think you should do it," I say. "I think you should stop doing drugs." He just laughs, thinking I'm kidding him. So I half quote one of the speeches from *The Fountainhead*, about human initiative, about success and the meaning of positive action, about the winner taking all, about going for it no matter what; soon I'm spouting any lame sports-type tagline I can think of just to make him realize he shouldn't be deciding anything right now. He reaches into his back pocket and takes the title to the Range Rover and signs the back of it.

"What should I say the sale price is?" he asks. I tell him to make it for fifteen; any less might raise a red flag with the tax people. He writes in $15,000 and hands it to me. Then he digs in his pocket and finds the parking garage ticket. We stumble out of the bar and walk a few blocks over to Mott Street to the concrete structure where Seth had stowed the vehicle. I pay the attendant and he hands me the key fob like it's mine, which now it is. The car is parked not far off, the way they always park the nicer cars on the ground floor, and I get behind the wheel and we tear out into the New York night.

I'm far too drunk to drive but we're not in an obedient mood, neither of us. Getting fired always is, for a time, a prudence minimizer.

We head south on the Bowery and then Seth directs me east to a place down near the PJs below the Williamsburg Bridge, off Ridge Street. This entails making a left turn on red and I negotiate it without a problem. Yogi Boy says the big-time deals on the LES are all brokered out of a dry cleaner's called El Jaguar.

"How do you know this shit?" I ask him and he says that anybody who ever bought drugs in New York knows Jaguar Dry Cleaners, it's legend.

"You can find a reference to it in like a hundred songs, from the Velvets to Snoop to the Strokes," he says. His energy is good now, he's up. Then he tries to sing a line from some track, it could be one of those bands he likes, Bum Bum Dudes or Illiteracy Society, I don't know.

"May the jaguar run / he goes on the ridge / May the jaguar run / down to the bridge." I don't know the song but the lyrics are suitably faux-secretive, the imparting of obscure drug-related insider knowledge one of the chief purposes of popular music throughout the ages. I am exhausted just thinking about all the young people in this city, their collective non-stop effort to be "hip," which is to say, to conform, to fit in, to Obey; all definitions in time come to mean their opposite. Why are people like this? Is it fear? Of what? Death? When Seth finishes singing we are pulling up in front of the store. He pats the envelope in his pocket and opens the passenger-side door; I search for the right line.

"I don't think this is a good idea," I say.

"I know," he says back to me. He hesitates for a moment before stepping out onto the curb and looking back at me behind the wheel. And then he turns and heads toward the storefront.

"Sethji," I call out. "Yo."

He turns back and looks at me, one hand on the door, the other gripping his cash. He's opened it about two inches and I can tell he doesn't really want to go inside, he's having

second thoughts, his forearm is trembling almost imperceptibly. "What?" he says.

"I was only kidding," I am saying to him as seriously as
I can.

"About what?"

"Dog, seriously," I go. "Don't do this."

"Do what?"

"Maybe you should take the money and use if for something else. Go to school."

"And study what?"

"I dunno, man," I say, this is new ground we're on. I pretend to scratch my head as an indication that I'm thinking out
loud, and of earnestness. "Maybe herbal medicine or something? Midwifery? Or go to law school, become a community
organizer? You know. Fight the power?"

He looks at me for a long time, like he can't tell if I am joking or not.

"Don't be an asshole," he says.

And then changing tone I say, "Just get in the car. I mean
it." He stands there for a second and I can tell he still doesn't
want to go inside but he's looking for an excuse so I lean over
and unlatch the passenger-side door and throw it open. He
takes this as a good enough cue and gets back in the car and we
sit there for a moment in utter silence. Then I take him home.

A few days later I have to return to the Tate offices in order to sign my severance papers; I get six months of pay and a year of benefits but because I breached my contract with an HR violation, they're giving me half that. Not bad. I take the subway to Thirty-fourth and walk to the Tate Worldwide building, panopticon of shame. I go to the benefits department and meet with a woman I had never seen before, her name is Angeline. I sign a bunch of papers without reading any of them and I go. No one greets me, no one notices me, no one says hello; this is my legacy after two years of toil. While I'm with Angeline I ask to use her phone and I dial Barry's number. He doesn't take my call. I dial HR Lady's number and she doesn't answer; I leave her a long message asking her if she got my e-mail or my fax or my text about compensating the people we fired with the bonus I was going to get and the one she surely will, about how is it people like us get seduced by this system, and how it's a shame but I always felt there was something between us, unspoken, and in different circumstances we might have meant something to each other. Then the voice cuts me off and asks me if I am satisfied with my message and I press 2: no. No, I am not satisfied with my message.

As I'm coming out of the building I see Henry Graham, my ex-colleague, lingering there across the street. I'm pretty sure he doesn't see me and so I have a few seconds to decide do I turn around in order to avoid him, do I keep going in order to avoid him, but then it's too late, he's right in front of me and looking right at me. I stop and smile at him and offer my hand. He doesn't take it.

"Henry," I say, shifting gears, "how are you?"

"Not bad, you?" he says. I keep my distance, thinking that if I were him I'd be punching me in the face now. But then I realize that a man in need of work doesn't entertain such thoughts around his former boss.

"I was going to e-mail you," I say, "but they shut off my account. I wanted to tell you that, um, it was pretty shitty what went on there and I'm, um, sorry about what happened."

"Oh sure, man," he says half-heartedly.

"They fired me, too, you know," I tell him. "Just a few days ago." Is this what a human would say? It occurs to me that it might be.

"Yeah, I saw that on Agency Spy," he says. I look down at his feet and see that he has bought some new John Fluevog boots: it's possible the man is trying to youngify himself. It's also possible he has begun to dye his hair, I can't quite tell in this light.

"How's it look out there?" I ask him, thinking that as out-of-work creatives we share something.

"Tough market, you know," he says with a shrug. "Tough market." I shrug back and we share a laugh, or should I say that I laugh in the hope he will join me.

"If I hear of anything, I'll let you know," I go. Still he says nothing. Then I ask him if he wants to have lunch.

"Now?" he says, looking at his watch.

"Why not?" I say. "On me."

I stand there and wait for him to answer. He looks around as if he's expecting to see someone he knows on the street, but he doesn't, and then smiles, more to himself than for my benefit, it seems to me. He grunts a strange kind of anxious grunt under his breath. Then he looks at me and I think he's going to say something, he's breathing in as if in anticipation of speaking, and then I see his hand go into his pocket and emerge holding what looks, for a second, like a gun, and I realize a nanomoment later something very interesting: it *is* a gun. A Beretta Tomcat Small Caliber Tip Out with a snag-proof design that permits quick presentation I was later told.

He's shaking it as he presents it at me.

"Henry," I say. "What are you doing?" I laugh the laugh of someone who doesn't fully believe he is standing in front of a desperate man holding a gun.

"Fuck you, Eric," he says. "You're a cunt."

"I know," I say. "I know that. Everybody knows that. Let's go eat."

For a moment I think it's worked, that he's going to put the gun away, or that I had only imagined it, that he never had a gun, that it was a phone.

But then he pulls the trigger of the gun and the trigger slams against the charge and the charge explodes in the narrow barrel, sending the necked-down Hornady V-Max .17 cartridge hurtling toward me. The tiny armor strikes me in the right side of my shoulder and I am knocked back a few feet but not to the ground.

A second explosion occurs and I feel nothing; this could be explained by the possibility that the bullet has hit me in the face and blown my head apart before I had a chance to feel it, but this is not the case: I feel nothing because he missed. Although there is a ringing in my ears.

Then he fires again, the third time being charmlike as the V-Max strikes me to the left of my solar plexus, a good hit, and as I am falling down and Henry Graham is running off down the sidewalk, people are scattering. My head hits the pavement and I black out.

I black out for what I later construe to be ten or eleven seconds; when I come to and look around, Henry is gone and there are people screaming and asking me if I am alive and then there are sirens, and cops, more screaming, more sirens, an EMS guy wearing plastic gloves that make him look like he works at a food truck, and then I'm moving, there are doors, hallways, men in blue shirts asking me questions, men with white masks talking to each other, needles, tubes, and very very bright lights.

One of the advantages of the midcentury modernist aesthetic is it's easy to pack up your things when you need to relocate, especially when you don't have any things. My moving company, called Green Transitions, is the first environmentally conscious moving company in New York (our boxes are made from recycled bamboo byproducts and our trucks run on bio fuels). As it happened, the first of Henry's tiny bullets had entered my shoulder muscle, luckily avoiding my humerus, scapula, and subscapularis, and exited cleanly out the back in a straight shot. The second hit above my abdomen, perforating the mesentery connecting my inferior vena cava to my small intestine, taking a sharp right and exiting without touching my spine, liver, or anything else of major value. Some call it a miracle. I call it a very informative eight days at New York Presbyterian followed by two weeks in bed watching every Preston

Sturges film there is on DVD, twice, I found his oeuvre quite compelling, it had been strongly recommended to me as therapeutic by Seth. "His approach to comedy is somewhat Buddhist," Seth informed me as we watched *The Great McGinty*, "seeing as how he refers to life as a 'cockeyed caravan,' which can be thought of as another term for samsara."

"Cool," I said. "Let's watch that one again."

Seth, carless and jobless, had gotten back together with his girlfriend, the one he thought was breaking up with him, and they told me they were starting this Etsy business together selling handmade hemp yoga mats, although they might have been joking, I couldn't tell.

Apart from a couple of visits from the two of them, and various food delivery people, and a few messages traded back and forth with my father, I didn't really talk to anyone, I wasn't after all in much of a social mood.

And then, finally, toward the end of week two, I got a series of texts pinging me in succession; they were from someone called BLOCKED.

OMFFFG!!?!!

i just heard about it i didnt do it i sware!! hope you are OK.

btw: *totally random violence* = so u ;),

but I wnted to say sorrysorry

eric

sorry i ran away @ the beach but you just didn't know the truth was i was fuck I was lying LYING

the whole time i was OMG am i telling u this? it was
tom
tom b who I met at the edit house who said i could
have a job if i f*ckd with your hed and at first
i did it because i just wanted to and
i am stupid and week and then I saw you and you
seemd so kewt and sad and everything hppened how
it did and then

i didnt know what to do i wanted to tell u
but then u told me u lovd me and so i ran awaay
i am sorry realy sorry that i did it and that i puked on
your house but i drank too music I mean too much
i love you *too* but too late for anything like that i know.
dont be hater - or do.... bye....
crying.......

(>_<)

I didn't text her back right away but then when I finally
did (*Sabi! call me!*) I realized I didn't know you could block
a cell phone but apparently you can and so therefore I had
no idea if my response even got to her, so I sent it again (*r u
kidding me? call me!!*) and then a third time (*pleez?!?*) but re-
ceived nothing in reply. I tried her old number but it was out
of service. Had she moved? I didn't know. I tried locating her
on Facebook but she had told me she wasn't even on Facebook and besides, I didn't know her last name. So I watched

movies and waited, and waited some more, and then one day I realized I could put my pants on without feeling like someone was stabbing me.

The last of my furniture is being taken into the freight elevator and the Green Transitions Relocation Team is loading it all into the truck. There are still two months left on my lease and I wasn't able to negotiate an early termination agreement to my liking so I'm just going to have to pay and leave the place empty. Now that everything is gone—I put the little cactus into my Rimowa suitcase last—I look out the east-facing windows at the skyline of Manhattan for a moment or two, it seems like the right thing to do as a sign-off. I count four private helicopters hovering above the East River; I take this as a sign that the economy is improving, but not for everyone.

For some reason I don't want to go, not just yet.

I have the rest of the afternoon free and consider paying Dr. Look a visit before I go, perhaps to discuss the feelings that I'm having about Sabine and her sudden and not completely surprising admission—I knew there was something weird about Tom—but otherwise I must admit it took me by surprise to have been played like that. Or perhaps I should just explain to Look that the story about my mom was fiction, the lie that tells the truth as it were, and that there are other stories I could have told him, that I could still tell. Then I dig out the card he gave me, it was in a folder of so-called important papers. I dial and a shrill voice tells me the number is out of service, please hang up and try again. I drop his card in the toilet and empty the last of my Xanax, Klonopin, Adderall, OxyContin, Percocet, Ativan, Zoloft, Wellbutrin, and Advil into the bowl and I flush. Then I grab my 1960s airline travel bag updated in Vachetta leather by Rag & Bone, consider turning off the bathroom light as I leave but don't, and walk out into the hallway where the elevators are. My phone rings and I can see by the 212 number it's the police precinct calling yet again; I had told them ad infinitum that I didn't get a good look at my assailant and couldn't even tell what race he was, or how tall, or what he was wearing, or if he was a woman, but something about my fabrication must have seemed to them like a lie because they keep persisting in questioning me about it. I decline the call for the very last time and head out of the building named Krave.

It's still raining as I drive west in the Range Rover. I left the city via the Holland Tunnel and picked up Interstate 80 in New Jersey off the turnpike, and that's when the rain started, in drizzly fits at first and then the sky was reduced to a smudge and the water came in long wailing bursts from all sides. The interstate's a more-or-less straight shot all the way to Chicago from here. Just past the Water Gap, in a town I see is called Bartonsville, PA, I stop for gas and check in with my device; no messages. My original thought was to drive all the way to Chicago in one very long day and night but the weather is slowing me down so around 6 PM I am still in central Ohio; soon I will be coming up on the Youngstown exit. My father had finally unloaded our childhood home a few years ago after he lost his shirt in the crash and moved to Florida. I decide it was only fitting, since I was going that way anyway, that I spend the night in the vicinity of where I grew up. And why push it? I had told my new employers at Draftfcb, where I will soon be one of two Executive Creative Directors on the Walmart account, that I wouldn't start until next week, so arriving a day later won't really make any difference to anyone. I've actually been to Chicago only once, not counting the times I've changed planes at O'Hare; I found it a charming if somewhat sleepy town. Draft is badly in need of a reboot and they had been bugging my headhunter Lynette for some time; after some wrangling I accepted the offer, promising to myself that this would be my last gig in the ad biz.

I pull off and get a room at the Quality Inn & Suites, it's only $59.99 a night. Not far down the access road is an Olive Garden Restaurant and I have a chef's salad, which was really nothing more than rolled up luncheon meats and four kinds of grated cheese in a creamy cheese-based dressing; I think if I looked hard I'd find some irradiated lettuce in there somewhere. I'm looking forward to getting to the Windy City and the interim corporate apartment they've got waiting for me in the River North section of town. After dinner I decide to drive around; Youngstown was a bustling working-class city not that long ago, a tree-lined paradise ringed with factories that made shoes and steel and, as I was intimately aware, the solenoids that went inside automobile fuel pumps. But this was back when we built things that people needed and used, things that had weight, things whose purpose was not just the enabling of fantasies, like Day-Glo NASCAR beer koozies, and those are made in Guangdong Province anyway (tagline: WE MAKE

REALITY THE MENTAL IDEAS YOU DO NOT KNOW YOU DREAM OF
BUT NEED FROM THE SADNESS).

It's still light and instead of going into Youngstown I find
myself driving west along Route 62, which when I was a child
was a country road but now is lined with golf courses and hast-
ily constructed strip malls featuring ninety-nine and ninety-
eight-cent stores. Canfield is a small Ohio town that quickly
became a suburb; the influx of southern blacks to Youngstown
in the 1950s, because of the prevalence of factory jobs, created
the need for a de facto whites-only enclave, and this is it. I remember the feeder streets well enough to find our subdivision,
which is called Forest Green Estates and had been carved,
ironically, from what had indeed been a forest but now the
landscape has been rendered almost entirely devoid of natural
vegetation. Each of the streets is named after a kind of tree or
shrub, some of which even existed at one time in the area; our
street was called Briarwood Lane. I turn right onto Bentwil-
low then left on Timber and then right on Briarwood and drive
slowly because I can't remember exactly what the number was.
Was it 84412 or was it 48812? Or something else entirely? I
get to the end of Briarwood, where it meets Chaucer (is that a
tree? who knew?), and realize I have the numbers wrong and I
must have driven past the place. I turn around (the RR's turning radius is impressive) and head back, going slower this time,
and then I recognize a house, or part of a house, the Mannings'
house, our former next-door neighbors. I say part of a house
because it wasn't really the Mannings' house anymore, it was
the Mannings' house transformed on steroids, as two massive,

oatmeal wings had been added to each side, and in the middle a vaulted ceiling had been grafted onto what once was the main part of the house, the whole concoction looking like an absurd half-finished mistake, something out of a graphic novel about the dystopian future. A sign on the lawn said the mutant home was for sale, and the chain and padlock on the front door indicated the bank had gotten involved and foreclosed on the whole atrocity midstream. To the left of the Mannings's ex-house there was an empty, muddy lot, actually an enormous muddy hole in the middle of an empty, muddy lot, and the hole was filled with brown, oily water. It wasn't square as it would have been if they were building a new home; the hole was kidney-shaped and long like a swimming pool, a swimming pool that was never finished, never filled in at last with cement, water, and joy. As I'm thinking this I look up and down the street, trying to picture my father there dealing with our dog, Race, on the day he was hit, and I realize that this empty hole is in fact where our house had stood, right there above that stagnant water. Our house was gone. Whoever it was who had bought the Mannings' place had bought ours, too, and had torn it down to make room for a pool, and then they had given up on the pool, and the renovation, if not a host of other dreams.

As it gets dark I decide to drive into Youngstown proper, as I haven't been back here since my father left, and see what else has changed. By the time I snake my way north and east through the bad neighborhoods and into the center of town, it's getting dark and I'm a little uncomfortable driving this kind of a car around here; although, getting carjacked by some tweaker on my way to a new job would be kind of poetic. As a kid we rarely came to town, apart from the occasional visit to my father's plant, which was several miles to the east, and it's like I'm seeing it for the first time. I cruise along Federal Street, which is the main drag, and nothing is open; I can't tell if this is a part of Youngstown on the way up or on the way down. I find a bar, a tavern on a corner, called the Brick House, and I park and go in. There's a handful of drunks and some other unsavory characters in there, an interesting cross between potheads and unemployed steelworkers, and a jukebox is alternating between old Slim Shady, Lynyrd Skynyrd, and Toby Keith.

I sit at the bar and order a Coke and within minutes a man with a boil on his forehead and an ass so big he needs two barstools is talking to me, asking me where I'm from; I tell him I grew up around here and am just back for a visit. For a couple of hours he doesn't stop going on, despite the fact I give him absolutely no signals that I am interested in his monologue whatsoever; but the fact that I'm buying his double vodkas is possibly motivating the performance, so I have only myself to blame. He is absolutely convinced of everything he tells me in the way that people who have never been anywhere outside the place where they grew up are convinced they know everything about everything. He is certain, for example, that an airplane never flew into the Pentagon, as certain as he is that the best Vietnamese food to be had anywhere outside of Hanoi, anywhere in the world, can be enjoyed right here in Youngstown, and that's because there were so many Vietnam vets (of which he is one) who survived the war and came back to town with their young Viet brides, and those girls, most of them quite attractive, they brought their entire families here with them to escape the goddam Communists, and many of the cousins opened up businesses, especially stores and restaurants, and they would open chop suey houses because that's what people around here thought of when they thought of gook food, chop suey and General Tso's Chicken and so on, but then this one family opened a bona fide Vietnamese establishment, very authentic, for the other Vietnamese people who were here, for their own community, it didn't even have a sign, but pretty soon it caught on, and got written up in the paper, and was hugely popular, and that family did well, and pretty soon all the other Vietnamese chop suey houses became real Vietnamese kitchens, too, that's how it happened, believe it or not. He also tells me, while on the inexhaustible subject of Y-town and its peoples, that the city could have been saved not long ago because there was going to be a blimp factory built just north of here, only the Socialists vetoed it, and that sealed the sad fate of their once-great region. This I also believe to be the truth, I tell him. His name is Frank, Frank Geshko or Leshko, he says finally, shaking my hand, and says it's the small gifts that we bestow on strangers that determine who we really are in the end, and I agree, saying isn't that the deep something or other we've all been yearning for? and he laughs as if he knows what I'm talking about and slaps me on the back. So I decide to tell him my own story: that in reality I work in advertising but was fired and that I'm driving by myself to Chicago to start my new life, which will most likely be a lot like my old life but who knows. He nods, sensing there's more to the tale, and so I tell him the whole sad story of a girl named Sabine, Sabi I called her, from the beginning, and how amazing she was, now that I think about it, and when I get to the part about the paranoia and the panic attacks and the shrink in the mental ward in Santa Monica asking me about my family, Frank stops me and asks why it was, when I saw the earlier psychiatrist, the fake one, that I told a crazy lie about my mom dying in a car crash? And then I just tell him, this Frank, this all-American male, I tell him all of it, the story of that summer when I was thirteen and we were living just up the road in a house that's a hole now, and how she had been diagnosed as manic-depressive, my mother, and how I remember some of the things she would do, and how my father couldn't understand her or where she was coming from, not that he tried, and they didn't have the medications in those days that they have today, and how she attempted to do it three times, or I should say two times, because on the third try she succeeded, and how I came upon her slumped in the corner of the upstairs guest bathroom, and how I noticed that she had tried to clean the blood off the (imported) Grigio Luna tile floor with a (monogrammed, imported) powder blue St. Etienne queen-size bath towel, tossing the by-then wine-dark fabric under the sink. Why had she tried to clean the floor of her blood? Did she in her last breath regret what she had done? Or only that she had made such a mess in doing it? Did she surmise that I would find her there and thought that, somehow, the impact would be less if the floor were clean(er)? Frank doesn't answer, he just stares at me and then breaks out laughing, hacking up gobs of phlegm and cat hair and chicken bones and god knows what else, saying he thinks I'm bullshitting him, and rather than put a damper on the night or confess to him that I've never told anyone that story, not quite like that, I just go, yeah Frank, my man, you're right dude, I'm a bullshitter, no sense trying to pull one off on the likes of you. He laughs and slams me on the back again like we're brothers in shame and struggle, and gets up and waddles off to take a piss; that's when I leave.

Before getting on the expressway the next morning I drive from the hotel back down to Federal Street to check it out in the daylight. I dig my digital Leica S2 out of my suitcase and cruise the streets photographing the empty storefronts and abandoned churches and boarded-up houses and small manufacturing plants near the railroad tracks. At one prominent corner I come upon a tremendous old theater, the Warner, which obviously hasn't been open for business in decades; I park in front and look around. From the sight of the jimmied-back plywood four-by-eights on the front doors I can tell there are people living in here. I had, after all, seen a number of what looked like former mental patients dragging themselves along these streets, shaggy white hair and beards, talking to themselves not unlike people with ear bobs on their Androids, and I assumed that at least some of that population might be living in the Warner. I go in carefully with my camera hidden in my jacket, and as I walk through the place I have to stop and listen for signs of life because the crackling of old linoleum and glass under my own feet gives me away.

In one corner of the lobby there's a door open to the basement but I'm afraid to go down there for fear of who I might wake up. I head up some wide curving stairs instead. I go through a leather-covered double door, and from the balcony of the theater I look down at the big old stage. Behind it there's a torn screen, stained from years of cigarette smoke, vomit, who knows what, most likely this was a porn theater in its latter days. Behind the blotchy screen are enormous red-velvet curtains that are ripped and water-stained at the bottom. Before showing adult movies it must have been some kind of legitimate culture palace, and I can imagine the place filled on a Saturday evening in the 1940s with the solid, kindly citizens of an American workingman's utopia, a place where, for the first and last time in human history, a good heart and a strong back would bring a man a reasonable amount of comfort and self-esteem during his short happy life; today, this man's grandchildren are thrice divorced and in rehab or jail. I keep going up the marble stairs covered in ripped and stained carpeting and finally get to a door. I don't know where the door leads but there's a table leg holding it open an inch or two and daylight is streaming in. I push open the door and I'm on the roof of the theater with views out across the great state of Ohio. I go to the parapet wall and look out. The sun is coming up to the east but I am turned the other way, west, toward the Great Plains and my new life ahead of me; who knows what it will entail. And then I see some kind of mist drifting in from the horizon, blurring the edges of everything, the roofs of the two flats below and the big-box stores farther out, with their empty parking lots, flat gray trapezoidal abstractions getting more and more out of focus, like a dust storm or a cloud of toxic gas covering everything, and then I realize it's not any of those things, it's me, it's my eyes doing it, it's my tears. I let them come.

I let them flow with me here on this ledge of destiny, naked, peering out across the glacier as Roark would do; it's so stupidly epic there are bells ringing in the distance. But then I wipe my eyes on my sleeve and realize the sounds are coming from my pocket. I pull out my phone and it's ringing and the screen says BLOCKED again.

I stare at the display for two-point-five rings in order to not seem too eager and then I answer.

"Hi," I say.